Books by E. D. Baker

THE TALES OF THE FROG PRINCESS:
The Frog Princess
Dragon's Breath
Once Upon a Curse
No Place for Magic
The Salamander Spell
The Dragon Princess
Dragon Kiss
A Prince among Frogs

———⊛———

Fairy Wings
Fairy Lies

———⊛———

TALES OF THE WIDE-AWAKE PRINCESS:
The Wide-Awake Princess
Unlocking the Spell
The Bravest Princess

———⊛———

A Question of Magic

A Tale of the Wide-Awake Princess

Unlocking
the
Spell

E. D. BAKER

BLOOMSBURY
NEW YORK   LONDON   NEW DELHI   SYDNEY

First published in the United States of America in October 2012
by Bloomsbury Children's Books
Paperback edition published in April 2014
www.bloomsbury.com

Bloomsbury is a registered trademark of Bloomsbury Publishing Plc

For information about permission to reproduce selections from this book, write to
Permissions, Bloomsbury Children's Books, 1385 Broadway, New York, New York 10018
Bloomsbury books may be purchased for business or promotional use. For information on bulk
purchases please contact Macmillan Corporate and Premium Sales Department at
specialmarkets@macmillan.com

The Library of Congress has cataloged the hardcover edition as follows:
Baker, E. D.
Unlocking the spell : a tale of the wide-awake princess / by E.D. Baker. — 1st U.S. ed.
p.   cm.
Sequel to: The wide-awake princess.
Summary: Princess Annabelle, who is immune to magic and can temporarily reverse spells
put on others, encounters various fairy tale characters when she embarks on an expedition
into the woods to find a dwarf responsible for turning Sleeping Beauty's prince into a bear.
ISBN 978-1-59990-841-0 (hardcover)
[1. Fairy tales. 2. Princesses—Fiction. 3. Magic—Fiction.
4. Characters in literature—Fiction.] I. Title.
PZ8.B173Un 2012   [Fic]—dc23   2012004223

ISBN 978-1-61963-194-6 (paperback)

Book design by Donna Mark
Typeset by Westchester Book Composition
Printed and bound in the U.S.A. by Thomson-Shore Inc., Dexter, Michigan
2 4 6 8 10 9 7 5 3 1

This book is dedicated to Ellie, my sounding board; to Kim, my research assistant; to Kevin, who is smarter than the average bear; to my fans for their support and enthusiasm; and to Victoria for her guidance and insight.

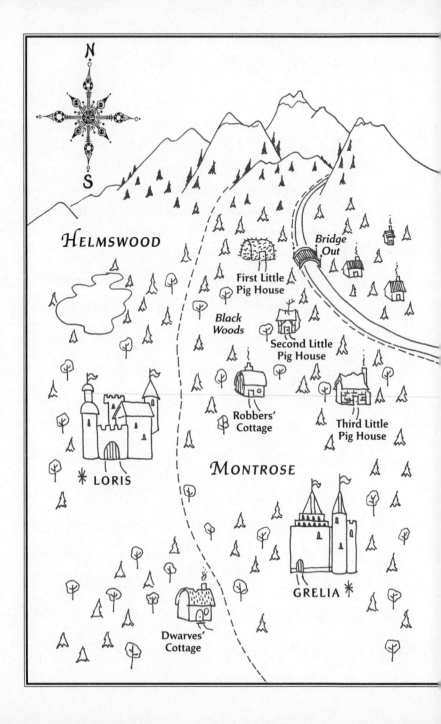

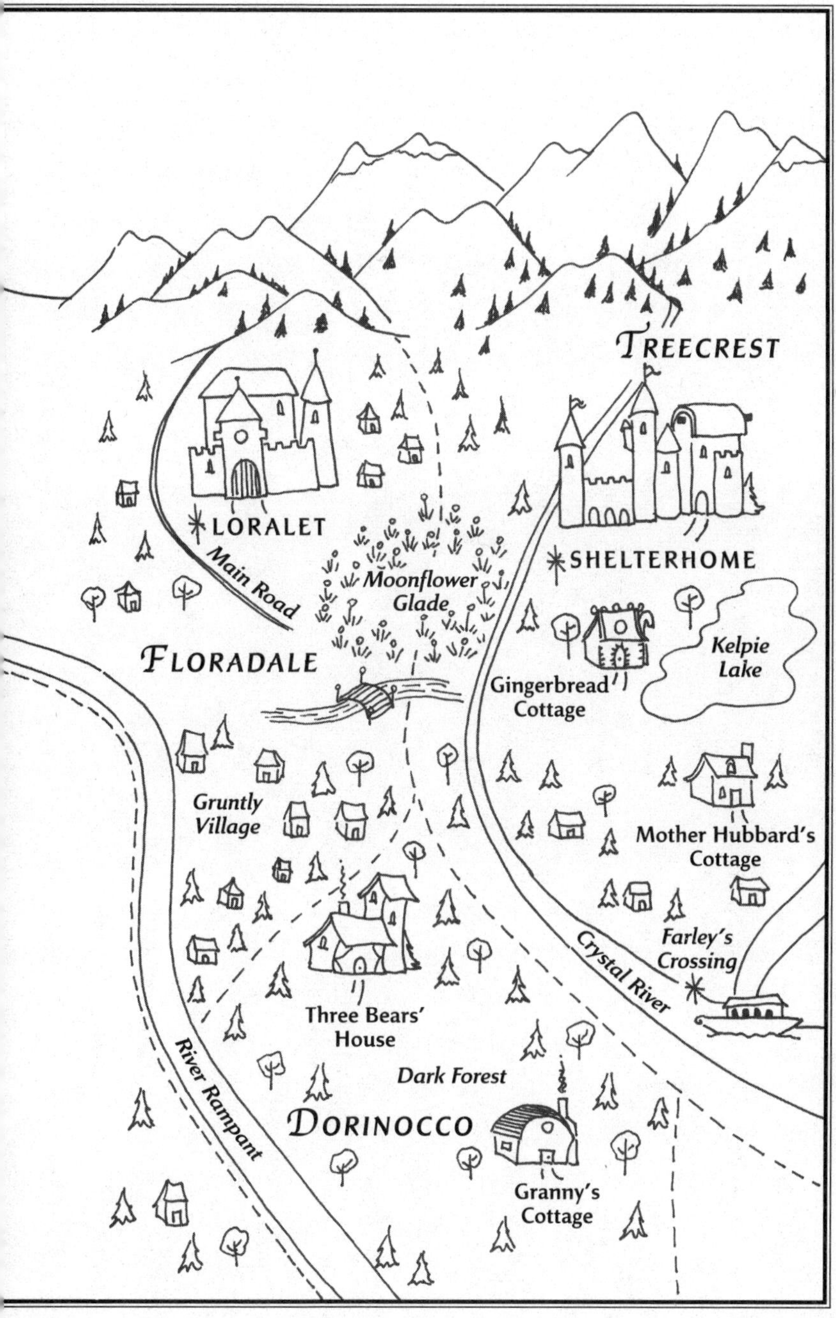
Treecrest
Loralet
Main Road
Moonflower
Glade
Shelterhome
Floradale
Kelpie
Lake
Gingerbread
Cottage
Gruntly
Village
Mother Hubbard's
Cottage
Farley's
Crossing
Crystal River
Three Bears'
House
River Rampant
Dark Forest
Dorinocco
Granny's
Cottage

Unlocking
the
Spell

CHAPTER 1

"Is THERE ANYONE ELSE?" Annie asked Horace, the gray-haired guard who was admitting petitioners to the room.

"Just one more, Your Highness," he replied. "A merchant named Bartley from Cobble on the Green."

Annie nodded. Most of the people who had come to see her that day had been merchants wanting to know if their gold was real. "How many visitors have I had altogether?"

"Two the first day, five yesterday, and twelve today. That would be nineteen, Your Highness. Word is spreading, so I imagine there will be even more tomorrow."

"I still can't believe this is happening," Annie said. "After all those years when most people didn't want me near them, they're coming from across the kingdom to ask for my touch. Who would have thought so many people would want magic removed so they could see what was really there?"

Annie glanced toward the window. All she wanted to do was go horseback riding along the river with Liam, but she'd told her parents she would meet with her petitioners before doing anything else. Of course, she had said that on the first day when only two had shown up. If she'd known there would be so many, she would have been tempted to refuse to see them at all—except she knew that she would have seen them no matter what. After all, Annie couldn't blame them for wanting to see the truth behind magic.

Shortly after Annie's birth, a fairy godmother had given her a special magic gift—no other magic could ever touch her. It wasn't long before her parents realized that with the gift came a special curse— anyone who touched her, or was near her for long, lost whatever magic they might have. It would come back once they were apart, of course, but in the meantime, those made beautiful and talented through magic became plain and ordinary. It was a truth not many wanted to face.

Annie turned toward the door when Horace opened it, admitting a short man with a rounded figure and a full head of graying hair. A pretty young woman with light brown ringlets and soft curves stood beside the middle-aged man. When the man bent low in a well-practiced bow, the young woman curtsied.

"Yes, Master Bartley?" Annie said with a sigh.

"Your Highness!" said the man, straightening up. "I know you're busy, but I won't impose on you for too much of your time. I just want to know one small thing. This is my betrothed, Ardith. We're getting married in a fortnight and I need to see if she's naturally this pretty or if magic made her this way."

"Bartley!" said the young woman. "You said she'd invited us here to give you a medal."

"Hush, Ardith!" Bartley told her, darting her an angry glance. "Not in front of the princess!" Turning back to Annie, he shrugged, saying, "She would have refused to come if I'd told her the truth. You see, I wouldn't have thought to bring her to see you if I hadn't seen a portrait of her grandmother. She was an ugly old hag, and I want to know if Ardith is going to give me ugly children."

"What an awful thing to say!" his betrothed said, her voice rising.

"Hold out your hand, Ardith," said Bartley, reaching for her.

Ardith snatched her hand away and stuck it behind her back. "I will not!"

As the couple engaged in a silent struggle, Annie glanced toward the window again when someone in the courtyard dropped a crate. Men shouted, and Annie wished she could peek out the window at the workers unloading newly arrived spinning wheels. But the way things were going, she could be stuck in that chair until nightfall, unless...

Annie slipped from her chair and approached the arguing couple. When she placed her hand on Ardith's shoulder, the young woman stopped fending off her future husband and stared at Annie in dismay. Bartley studied Ardith, his mouth set in a grim line, and didn't notice when Annie placed her other hand on *his* shoulder.

It took only a few moments for the changes to begin. Although Ardith's face stayed as pretty as when she'd first walked in, her body lost its curves and became bony and angular. At the same time, the hair on Master Bartley's head disappeared, leaving his scalp pink and shiny, while tufts of hair sprouted from his ears and his eyebrows grew straggly on either side of his suddenly large, hooked nose. When he opened his mouth, his teeth were as uneven as a willow-wand fence after a big storm.

"Huh!" Bartley said, looking Ardith up and down. "Well, at least you didn't turn ugly. You'll do, I suppose."

Ardith gasped and her eyes grew wide. "But you won't do at all! You accused me of improving my appearance through magic when you did the same thing yourself. And then to put me through this..." Her breath caught with a hitch as she turned and ran from the room.

"Ardith!" Bartley called as he followed her out the door.

"He didn't even say thank you," Annie said, and broke into a grin. "Horace," she added, turning to the guard. "That's enough for today. If anyone else shows up, tell them to come back tomorrow."

"Of course, Your Highness," he said, and grinned back at her.

❦

Annie was hurrying to the stable, hoping to meet Liam there, when she ran into a group of minor nobles come to pay their respects to the king of Treecrest. For years visitors had been turned away for fear that they might sneak spinning wheels into the castle in order to put everyone inside to sleep. Now that Annie's sister, Gwendolyn, had woken from the spell and spindles could no longer hurt her, King Halbert had lost no time importing the wheels by the hundreds. The kingdom was once again facing prosperity, and visitors from other kingdoms were flocking to the castle, hoping to earn favor with the king.

A man dressed in a fur-trimmed cloak despite the pleasant weather looked up as Annie tried to wend her way through the group blocking the stable door. "You, girl, fetch us drinks. Can't you see that we're parched from our travels?"

"Annie, there you are!" Gwendolyn's musical voice called from the center of the group. "I've been looking all over for you."

Annie wasn't sure which was worse—having a stranger mistake her for a serving girl, or having her sister find her. She thought briefly about running away from both, but that would be cowardly. Even so... Annie groaned when she spotted Gwendolyn coming toward her and realized that she'd hesitated too long.

"Lord Abernathy, you must meet *my sister, Princess* Annabelle," Gwendolyn said, directing the man in the fur trimmed cloak toward Annie.

"Your sister...," he said, his Adam's apple bouncing in his throat when he swallowed hard. "I do apologize, Your Highness. The sun must have been in my eyes."

"I understand," said Annie, even as she tried to edge away from Gwendolyn.

Annie wasn't surprised that the man hadn't known she was a princess; unlike the princesses made beautiful through magic, she was as normal as the day she was born. Gwendolyn was the most beautiful princess in all the kingdoms with her buttercup-yellow hair and violet eyes, but Annie's hair was sun-bleached blond, her eyes were ordinary brown, and, after spending so much time in the sun while looking for a prince to kiss her sister, she now had more than her fair share of freckles.

As much as Annie found her sister's perfection

irritating, it was even more galling that Gwendolyn had suddenly become nicer and more caring than she ever used to be. Before she pricked her finger on the spindle of a spinning wheel and fell asleep, Gwennie wouldn't have noticed the way the nobleman had slighted her sister. But after Annie worked so hard to break the curse, her family's attitude had changed as if they knew how much they owed her and how much she really loved them. They no longer treated her like a poor relative and actually acted as if they liked her, a development that never failed to surprise Annie. It also reminded her how badly they'd behaved toward her before.

For most of Annie's life, Gwendolyn had kept her distance from her sister, not wanting her fairy-given beauty to fade. But now that Gwennie was in love with an enchanted prince who'd been turned into a bear, she no longer seemed to care about her own appearance as much as she had before. She even sought Annie out at times, wanting her sister to touch the bear prince and lessen the magic of the enchantment so his human side could show through. Gwennie never seemed to notice that Prince Beldegard looked like a strange half-human monster when he was partway changed. His appearance didn't bother Annie, but she was so tired of sitting around with her hand on a not-quite-human-looking man who was kissing her sister that she'd begun to look back with a certain fondness on the days that she'd been shunned.

She was remembering how it used to be before so much had changed when Lord Abernathy cleared his throat and said, "If this is your sister, then she's..."

When he stepped back with a sudden look of panic in his eyes, Annie saw that he was aware of her reputation; this was the princess whose touch made magic fade. Not everyone had changed their minds about being around Annie.

"If you'll excuse us," Gwendolyn told Lord Abernathy. Nodding to his traveling companions, she ushered Annie around the side of the stable to a place they could be alone. "I have to talk to you," she said. "The woodsmen are back without seeing any sign of the awful dwarf who turned my Beldegard into a bear. Mother and Father promised that we would help him, but we can't do anything unless we find that dwarf."

"Yes, I know," Annie said.

"And you know I can't marry him until the spell is broken."

"Uh-huh," said Annie.

"Then you must know that you have to help us! Beldegard and I love each other, but we can't go on this way! Every time I want to kiss him, or hold his hand, or gaze into his *human* eyes, I have to run all over the castle looking for you so you can sit with us, holding *my* prince's other hand so he can be his human self."

"Believe me, I know that, too," said Annie.

"You brought Beldegard to me, so you're responsible

for this. I know you did it to wake me and save the kingdom, but I never would have known that he was my one true love if you hadn't introduced us. Surely you must feel some sort of obligation to help us?"

"What you don't seem to remember is that I came home less than a week ago from traipsing all over the countryside looking for princes to kiss you, hoping you would wake up and our lives could get back to normal. The last thing I want to do is go looking for someone else! I want to enjoy just being here with everyone awake and talking, instead of lying there looking like they're dead!"

"I know how dreadful it must have been for you," Gwendolyn said, looking so concerned that Annie felt a twinge of guilt, "but won't you please reconsider?"

"I'll think about it," Annie grumbled, and walked off, trying not to picture the tears that she had seen pooling in her sister's eyes. She thought about suggesting that Beldegard and Gwennie go without her, but she knew that the bear prince had been fruitlessly searching for the dwarf for years and Gwennie was too used to being pampered to be of much help. The best person to go would be someone who wouldn't mind stomping though the woods and whom the dwarf couldn't change with his magic. Even Annie had to admit that only one person fit that description: Annie herself.

Chapter 2

Annie waited at the edge of the drawbridge as the last heavily loaded wagon crossed into the castle courtyard. She enjoyed the rumbling of the wheels as they rolled over the wooden boards, and the way the sound changed as they reached the stones of the courtyard itself. Annie had never been as conscious of sound as she was now. Being awake in a castle where everyone else was sleeping had made her appreciate the little things, like a child's laughter, a dog's bark, and voices rising and falling with the ebb and flow of conversation. Although silence had never bothered her before, too prolonged a silence now made her uneasy.

Once the drawbridge was empty of everyone but a messenger on horseback and a few people on foot, Annie hurried across, anxious to talk to Liam. A hostler in the stable had told her that he'd seen Liam asleep under the tree on the other side of the road, but when she finally spotted him, he was sitting up, smiling as she crossed the dusty road to sit beside him.

"There were too many people in the courtyard, so I came out here for some peace and quiet," said Liam, taking her hand in his. "How was your morning?"

"Long," she replied with a grimace. "I've become popular with merchants who want to see if their gold is real. I feel sorry for some of them; they came with sacks of gold and left knowing that many of the coins were base metals that looked like gold because of magic."

"I wouldn't feel too sorry for them if I were you," said Liam. "The first thing those merchants will do is foist those coins off on someone else. Are you tired of seeing petitioners yet?"

"Yes, but I'm more tired of sitting beside Gwennie and Beldegard every time they want to gaze into each other's eyes and talk about how much they love each other. This morning they invited me to join them for breakfast just so they could make moon eyes while I gobbled my porridge. Do you still want to go for a horseback ride? There's time before supper if we go now. We could ride down to the river and—"

"I tell you, it's her!" said a flower fairy as four of the little creatures flew down to hover just above Annie's head.

"Not again!" Annie groaned as the fairies flew so

close that she almost went cross-eyed looking at them. Glancing from one to another, she wondered what they were waiting for.

"Did you see that?" crowed a fairy wearing the feathery leaves of a fern. "She's shifty eyed, just like they said."

"Who's shifty eyed?" Annie said, leaning back so she could see them better.

"You!" they all said at once.

"We've come to challenge you to a contest of magic," said a male fairy in a bluebell cap. "Our magic is stronger than anything you can do, and we are going to prove it."

"You might want to get out of the way," Annie told Liam as all four fairies raised their magic wands. Keeping her eyes on the fairies, she waited until she heard Liam jump to his feet and step aside. "Go ahead, do your worst," Annie said without even bothering to stand.

In an instant, the fairies aimed their wands at her and fired. Sparkling lights shot from the wands, hit Annie with a shivery, bright sound, and rebounded back into the fairies' faces. The fairy on the right began to spin in place until she was just a blur. The nose of the fairy beside her grew long and her feet turned into those of a duck. The skin of the fairy in the bluebell cap was suddenly covered with multicolored spots, but the fairy wearing fern leaves just got prettier with her shaggy hair curling softly around her face, her eyes getting larger, and her pudgy body becoming slender and curvy.

When the fairy who was spinning stopped, she brushed the tangled hair out of her face and glanced from Annie to her friends. Spotting the fairy wearing ferns, she glared at her saying, "What spell did you use, Fern? We were all supposed to do something awful to her! What kind of challenge is it if your magic would have made her prettier?"

Fern shrugged and looked away.

"She was hedging her bets, that's what she was doing!" said the fairy in the bluebell cap. "She used a beauty spell in case it really did bounce back like everyone said it would."

"Well, why not?" said Fern. "Look at me, then look at you!" The fairy snorted and burst out laughing at the expressions on her friends' faces.

"You little traitor!" cried the fairy with the duck feet, and they all three took off after Fern, who sped away still laughing.

"Has this been happening a lot?" Liam asked as he and Annie watched the tiny fairies skitter around flowers and trees until they disappeared from sight.

"More than I care to remember," said Annie. She sighed and rubbed her temples with her fingertips, trying to ease the headache that was forming. "The fairies can't seem to believe that magic doesn't work on me. I'm getting so tired of this. Ever since we came back, people have been hounding me for one thing or another. I'm almost tempted to do what Gwennie wants and take Beldegard to look for his dwarf just so I can get away from the favors and the challenges and the vile looks from people like Lord Abernathy."

"Who?" said Liam.

Annie gave him a half smile and shook her head. "No one important."

"Let's go for that ride now," Liam said, taking Annie's hand and pulling her to her feet. "A gallop along the river is just what you need."

Annie laughed as he pulled her close. He was just about to kiss her when someone gave a polite cough behind them. Startled, Annie turned around.

An older woman with a red face and blade-thin nose was watching her from only a few feet away with a younger version of herself by her side. Before Annie could say anything, the woman swept her an abrupt curtsy, then pointed at one of the guards standing by the foot of the drawbridge. "That guard told me who you were. I know you weren't going to see any more petitioners today, but I was sure you'd make an exception for us, seeing that we came from so far away. I'm Maeve, and this is my daughter, Becca."

Annie sighed. Sometimes it was easier to help people than to put them off until another day. "How can I help you?" she asked.

"When my daughter was born she was colicky and

cried all the time. A passing fairy took pity on me and cast a spell making Becca's voice as sweet as a lullaby. It was all right when she was a baby, but well, you'll have to hear for yourself. Becca?"

The girl opened her mouth, and out came a lovely voice, sweet and melodious, singing the words, "I cannot talk, I only sing, and everything I sing is sweet. My voice puts everyone to sleep."

Annie glanced at Liam when he took a loud, prolonged breath and yawned. His eyes were already half closed when Becca finished singing.

"We thought that since you had experience with this kind of thing, you might be able to help us," said Maeve.

"I'm afraid you're mistaken. I've never dealt with anything like this before. It wasn't singing that put the people in the castle to sleep and it took a very particular kind of magic to wake them. My touch will stop a spell from working, but only temporarily."

Maeve glanced at Becca, then back at Annie. "That should be enough."

Becca nodded. "Even a minute with a normal voice would be enough for me," she sang. "I just want to know what it would be like to talk instead of sing."

Annie noticed that one of Liam's eyes fluttered shut. The other eye looked as if it was about to close as well. Annie reached for Becca's hand.

"How long does this take?" the girl sang, but even as

the last word crossed her lips, her voice lost its lilt. "Is this my real voice?" she said, her voice becoming flatter and taking on a whiny edge. With a gleam in her eye, Becca turned toward her mother. "I blame you for all of this, Mother. If you hadn't complained about me to every Tom, Dick, and fairy who passed by, this would never have happened. Lots of mothers have to deal with colicky babies without a fairy's magic! I can't believe my own mother—"

Maeve took Annie's hand from Becca's, saying over her daughter's voice, "That was enough. At least now we know what we were missing. Thank you, Your Highness. Let's go home, Becca."

Her daughter's voice sounded more melodious just moments after Annie stopped touching her. "I can't sing anything that isn't nice, no matter how hard I try," Becca half sang. "It's so frustrating!" she trilled. When she heard herself sing, Becca closed her mouth and began to pout.

"I don't know which of them I feel sorrier for," Annie told Liam as the mother and daughter walked away.

Liam glanced at the drawbridge and nudged Annie. "Look at all the people coming our way. I bet they want to talk to you, too."

Annie groaned when she saw the approaching crowd. "If I stay here, I may never have another minute to myself. Taking that trip with Beldegard is becoming more tempting by the minute, but only if you come, too."

A guard pushed through the crowd and reached Annie first. "Your Highness," he said, "His Majesty, the king, requests your presence."

"So much for going riding," Annie told Liam.

"Do you want me to go with you?" he asked.

"You might as well. My father likes you and I doubt he has anything to say that he won't want you to hear."

༄

When they reached the king's private audience chamber, Annie's father wasn't the only one there. Queen Karolina was seated beside the king, while Princess Gwendolyn stood next to her with her hand resting on the head of a huge black bear.

"You know we all appreciate everything you have done, Annabelle," said the king once she and Liam stood before him.

Annie nodded, wondering why her father wanted to thank her once again. "However," he said, and her heart sank. Now she was sure this couldn't be anything good. "It has come to my attention that you have refused to help your sister's betrothed. Both your mother and I have promised Prince Beldegard that our family will help him break the spell that turned him into a bear so that he can marry your sister. As our daughter, you are obligated to help us fulfill our promises."

Annie frowned and glanced at her sister, who she

thought looked insufferably smug. "I'll go," Annie told him, "but I get to choose who goes with me."

"Agreed," said the king, sounding relieved.

Gwendolyn opened her mouth, and closed it without speaking. Annie thought her sister no longer looked quite so smug.

CHAPTER 3

THE NEXT DAY, Annie rose early and dressed in the clothes of a stable boy, just as she had when she went in search of a prince for Gwendolyn. Annie had learned long ago how much easier it was to walk through the deep woods when she wasn't wearing a long, trailing gown, and she liked the sense of freedom of the less-constricting boys' clothes. She thought it made more sense to travel as a boy, too. People were less likely to figure out who she was and ask her to do things for them. After gathering a boy's cap to cover her hair, a change of clothes, a thin blanket, a knife, and some coins, she hurried down to the kitchen for food.

Annie had always been the more practical sister. In keeping their distance from their younger daughter, her parents had been sparing in their time and affection, so she'd learned how to do a lot of things herself. From a young age, she had spent long hours with the children of servants and lesser nobles who didn't have much magic to lose. Spending time with them often meant watching their parents at work. She learned how to churn cream into butter, clean out a fireplace, examine a horse to see why it was lame, and make knots that would last for years. She knew how to take inventory of all the supplies in the kitchen, plan the provisions needed in case of a siege, interview new workers, fire the incompetent, be firm with tradesmen, and give orders that would be followed immediately. Although she couldn't dance as beautifully or sing as sweetly as a princess who been made talented through magic, Annie had mastered many skills that magically gifted princesses could never hope to possess. For someone as levelheaded as Annie, an expedition into the woods to find a nasty, magic-wielding dwarf wasn't at all intimidating.

❧

By the time Annie reached the courtyard, Liam was already waiting for her with his satchel at his feet. Although Annie usually had a sunny disposition in the morning, she felt cross and out of sorts. "What's wrong?" he asked when he saw her expression. "You look like your dog died."

"I don't have a dog," she said, sounding surly. "And nothing's wrong. It's just that my father is making me do this."

"I don't understand," said Liam. "If you'd already decided to help Beldegard, why does it bother you so much that your father ordered you to go?"

Annie shrugged. "It's one thing if you plan to do something yourself, but it feels different if someone tells you to do it, especially if you already made up your mind about it. Hasn't that ever happened to you?"

"I suppose," said Liam.

"It doesn't matter, though," Annie told him. "I still have to go. At least I get to choose who goes with me," she said, her expression brightening.

"Are you sure Beldegard and I will be enough? Your father offered to send as many soldiers and servants as you wanted. I know he and your mother aren't happy that you aren't taking any."

Annie shook her head. "The three of us will be fine. Beldegard says that the dwarf is in the forest south of here. If we're lucky, finding him won't take long, but if we drag too many people with us we might scare him off."

"And if we're unlucky?" said Liam.

"Then we'll need to go farther to find him. If that happens, we'll be able to move faster with fewer people."

"Your sister wasn't nearly as upset as I thought she'd be when you said she couldn't go."

"I know," said Annie. "That's what has me worried. Either it means that she doesn't love Beldegard the way I thought she did, or she has something planned. I've never known her to give up so easily when she really wants something."

"Why didn't you want her along?"

"Because when Gwennie does anything, everything always has to be about her. If we're going to find the dwarf, we're not going to have time to cater to my sister. Besides, part of the reason I wanted to go was so I wouldn't have to hold Gwennie's and Beldegard's hands while they kissed. I'm sick and tired of it!"

"I didn't know it bothered you so much," Beldegard said in his deep, scratchy voice as he padded across the cobblestones. "Sorry I'm late. I was just saying good-bye to Gwendolyn."

Annie glanced from the bear prince to her sister, who was walking beside him with her hand on his head as if he were a big dog. "You're not going with us," Annie told her.

"I just came to say good-bye again," Gwendolyn replied. "Oh, Beldegard, I'm going to miss you," she cried, throwing her arms around the bear prince's neck.

"I'm going now," Annie announced, turning toward the drawbridge. "Anyone who wants to go with me who isn't named Gwendolyn had better hurry. Come on, Liam," she said as she began to run.

"Slow down, this isn't a race," Liam called, and sprinted after her. "Don't we need Beldegard to show us where to start looking?" he asked when he caught up.

"I wasn't about to wait around while they said

good-bye *again*," said Annie. "Gwennie would want me to hold Beldegard's paw so she could kiss him. The way those two act we might not get started until noon. We'll head toward the forest. Beldegard will catch up with us sooner or later."

They had just reached the forest when they heard the sound of thudding feet behind them. Annie turned and smiled when she saw the bear prince galloping across the open field, moving faster than most horses. Her smile faded when she spotted Gwendolyn on the parapet, waving a handkerchief in the air. "Oh, brother," Annie said as she turned away.

"Where did you want to look first?" Liam asked the bear prince.

"Where I saw the dwarf last," Beldegard said, sounding grim. "A few miles from the old widow's cottage. It's not far from where I first met you and Annie."

"Then we have a long walk ahead of us today," said Annie.

Liam glanced at Beldegard. "I still wish we could ride there. Are you sure horses couldn't go where we're headed?"

"I'm sure," said the bear prince. "You'd have to abandon them when the going gets rough."

"One other thing," said Liam. "Before we go any farther, I just want to know if you're sure this particular dwarf was the one who changed you. I mean, couldn't it have been a fairy or a witch?"

Beldegard snorted and shook his head. "We were arguing when the dwarf raised his hand and said something about me being a bear. The next thing I knew, I was standing on four paws craving fish. That was enough proof for me."

"Sounds convincing," said Liam.

As they made their way through the forest, Annie was careful to keep her distance from Beldegard, not because he was a bear, but because she wanted him to stay that way. She knew that he found it difficult to walk when he began to change and his feet were neither bear paws nor human, so when Beldegard wasn't ranging ahead, she walked with Liam between them.

They were following the road through the trees when they passed a woodcutter and his wife heading into town. After that, they walked for hours without seeing anyone else. It was nearly lunchtime when they ran into an old woman sitting by herself on a large rock at a crossroad. She glanced at them, her gaze sliding over Annie, to Liam and the bear prince, then darted back to the princess, her eyes alight with excitement. "It's you!" she exclaimed.

"Oh, yuck," Liam said as a snake slithered from between the old woman's lips.

The woman spit and wiped her mouth with the back

of her hand. "I was hoping you'd come this way again!" she told Annie. Her mouth widened and a frog crawled out to plop onto her lap. She brushed it off, then raised a crooked finger.

Frogs, snakes, and lizards poured from the old woman's mouth as she screamed at Annie. The writhing creatures half filling her mouth made her words sound garbled, but Annie could hear when magic was present and she could just make out the snippet of a raspy tune. Suddenly a bright light shot from the woman's finger, hit Annie, and bounced back, smacking the woman in the face so that she fell off the rock, sputtering.

When the old woman scrambled back onto the rock, her expression was exultant. "I did it!" she said, sounding gleeful, but even before the last word was out of her mouth, a frog tumbled onto the ground and a stream of pearls dribbled from her lips.

The old woman looked confused. "What was...?" she said, then clapped her hand over her mouth. Her fingers separated as a slow-moving lizard peeked out. The old woman's hand was shaking when she pulled the lizard from her mouth, flinging it into the forest. Rose petals fluttered from her lips to the ground. "That wasn't supposed to happen!" she cried, spewing a shower of pearls, tadpoles, and slimy green snakes. Looking horrified, she jumped to her feet and scurried down the path.

"What was that all about?" Liam asked.

"I think she wanted to replace the spell she tried to use on me the last time we met," said Annie. "It looks as if she just added pearls and rose petals to the lizards, snakes, and frogs."

Beldegard nudged a frog with his paw, sending it hopping into the woods. "I'd hate to have that spell aimed at me."

"Right," muttered Liam. "Because being a bear is so much better."

"What did you say?" Beldegard asked him.

"I was just wondering how much farther we have to go," Liam told him.

"We're about halfway there," said the bear prince. "No more paths for us now. I'll lead the way."

"Good," Annie said as they began to walk. "Maybe we won't meet anyone else who recognizes me."

❦

They made good time with Beldegard in the lead. He knew the forest well and took them down deer trails and along streambeds. When underbrush blocked their way, he plowed through, making a trail of his own.

Traveling with him was faster than Annie's first trip south, so they came upon the witch's gingerbread cottage while it was still daylight. It didn't look at all the way she remembered it. The roof had collapsed and rain had half dissolved the walls. Animals had nibbled the sections that were left and the ground around it was crisscrossed with paw prints of all sizes. None were larger than Beldegard's, however, and when he went close enough to peer through a gaping window, two wolves raised their heads and slunk away.

While Annie looked inside for signs of what might have happened to the old witch who had lived in the cottage, Liam examined the ground outside. It didn't take long to see that Granny Bentbone was gone, along with the magic that had held the cottage together. Annie was still wondering what had become of the old woman when Liam joined her.

"No dwarves have been here as far as I can tell. The only shoe prints are yours and mine," he told her. "Hey, Beldegard, does your dwarf wear shoes?"

The bear prince shuffled closer. "Little shoes with pointy toes. They were made with leaf imprints on the bottom, so they were easy to track."

"Nothing like that around here," said Liam.

Beldegard whuffed and said, "I wasn't really expecting there would be. I usually found his tracks near water. There's a lake not far from here."

It was dusk when once more they followed the bear prince through the woods. When Annie spotted a ring of mushrooms that might have been where she'd danced with the fairies, she walked faster, not wanting to see them again. Only a few minutes later they reached the edge of the lake, but it was already too dark to look for footprints.

"We'll stay here for the night and start looking again first thing in the morning," Beldegard announced.

"I don't think we should stay so close to the water," Liam told him, casting a suspicious glance toward the lake. "There's no way of knowing what might come out of that water at night."

"Isn't this the lake where we saw the kelpie?" Annie asked him.

Liam glanced at her and nodded, his mouth set in a pinched line. Annie had rescued him from the horselike monster. It was an unpleasant memory.

"Don't worry!" said Beldegard. "No kelpie has been born that would challenge me! We'll be perfectly safe. Liam, move those rocks and put your campfire there. You can unroll your blankets on the other side."

Liam scowled at the bear. "I don't recall anyone appointing you leader of this expedition."

Beldegard snorted. "Of course I'm the leader. *You're* helping *me*, remember?"

"Yes, but you're a bear," said Liam.

"Which means I'm better suited to lead," the bear replied. "I'm bigger than you and stronger and look far more fearsome. No one will mess with us while I'm in charge."

"Maybe, but that just means you'd make a great guard. A good leader needs to be smart, and, well, you're a bear."

Beldegard narrowed his eyes and curled his upper lip, exposing his pointed teeth. "Are you calling me stupid?" he asked, his voice a low growl.

"Not at all," Liam replied. "Although letting yourself get turned into a bear probably wasn't the smartest thing you've ever done."

"Why you little...," Beldegard roared, rising onto his hind legs so that he towered over Liam. "I ought to—"

"Calm down," said Annie stepping between the two princes. "Fighting each other isn't going to get us anywhere. Liam, I'd appreciate your help starting a fire. And you, Beldegard... would you go look for berries? Some fresh fruit would be nice with dinner." All Annie wanted to do was have a bite to eat and curl up in a blanket beside the fire, but it didn't look like she was going to do either as long as the two princes were fighting.

The bear prince growled even as he plopped down on all four paws. Grumbling under his breath, he shambled off into the underbrush.

Liam glanced at the water gently lapping the shore only a short distance away. "I don't care what the bear says, I'm not going to get a wink of sleep if we stay here."

"Then why don't you look for another camping place

for us where you *will* be able to sleep," suggested Annie. "It's getting dark, but if you hurry you might be able to find something."

Liam's expression brightened. "Good idea. I'll find us a likely spot and come get you. Don't unpack anything yet. I'll be right back."

As Liam disappeared into the gloom under the trees, Annie set her knapsack on the ground. Her stomach had been grumbling for some time now, and she was tempted to finish off a hunk of bread left over from lunch, but she thought she really should wait for Liam to return. She yawned and rubbed her eyes. When she opened them the twinkling lights of a dozen fairies were flitting through the trees.

"Look, it's the girl who wouldn't dance with us!" cried a fairy. "Can you believe she had the nerve to come back here?"

Annie sighed. The last time she'd been in these woods, the fairies who lived here had pinched and poked her when they saw that their magic had no effect on her. She was too tired to fend them off tonight, but it looked as if she might not have a choice.

When something splashed far out in the lake, Annie glanced toward the water. She was sure she had frightened the kelpie the week before when she had pulled Liam from its back, so she didn't think it would be eager to face her again.

A fairy darted close enough to pull her hair. "Pay attention when we're talking to you! Unless…are you afraid of something out there? Maybe we don't have to teach her a lesson again," the fairy said as its friends darted closer. "Maybe we can get someone else to do it for us."

The rustle of leaves and snap of a twig announced someone's approach through the underbrush. Tiny lights twinkled as the fairies flew toward the lake. Annie watched them go, then turned back when Liam said, "I found a better camping spot. It's far enough from the water that—"

Something too big to be a fish splashed in the lake. Liam was already pulling his sword from its scabbard when Annie spotted the kelpie's head cutting through the water. As it reached the shallows and waded to the shore, Annie could see the beast more clearly. It was too dark to be sure, but it appeared to be the same one that had carried Liam into the lake to drown him.

The beast nickered when fairies zipped around it, turning its head toward Annie. When the kelpie left the water, it looked so much like a normal horse that Annie could see how Liam had been deceived. With its eyes fixed on Annie, the kelpie slowed and lowered its head, its ears twitching in her direction. It wasn't until the beast drew close enough to smell her that it pinned back its ears and snarled.

"Get away from her!" Liam shouted, charging the kelpie with his sword in his hand. Annie backed away when the kelpie reared and lashed out with its hooves. Liam's sword sliced the air as he darted toward the kelpie, ducking out of the way of the striking animal. The beast veered after him, twisting its neck in a snakelike move and clashing its teeth only inches from Liam's back. Fairies cheered until Liam dropped to the ground and rolled, bringing around his sword to nick one of the striking legs. The kelpie screamed even as Liam turned and, with his sword whistling through the air, drove the kelpie into the lake.

Fairy lights darted out over the water as the little creatures tried to urge the kelpie back into battle. The kelpie's nostrils flared, its sides heaving as it faced Liam from the shallows. The prince was standing with his legs braced, his sword held high, when Beldegard burst from the underbrush, chuffing. Reaching the edge of the water, the bear prince rose to his hind legs and bellowed. Fairies scattered, fleeing into the woods, while the kelpie danced back, spun on one hind hoof, and plunged into the deeper water, disappearing beneath the surface so that only ripples betrayed where it had been.

Beldegard was chuckling as he dropped to all fours and turned toward Annie. "See, I told you the kelpie would be afraid of me."

"Actually, I think Liam was doing a very good job

before you got here," Annie told him. Liam glanced up from wiping his sword with a handful of leaves, and grinned at her.

"Hunh," the bear prince snorted.

"It looked as if the fairies were afraid of you, too, just like the last time we were here," Annie said to Beldegard. "Why do you suppose that is?"

"I can't imagine," he said, sitting down on his haunches and using a claw to pick his teeth.

"You didn't eat one, did you?" said Annie, appalled.

Beldegard shrugged. "Sometimes bears get distracted by pesky little nuisances and eat things that aren't actually berries."

A small scream made Annie jump as a single fairy light streaked away. "I guess you upset their spy." She turned back to the bear prince, looking thoughtful. "If the fairies are afraid of you, maybe they won't pester me when we're together. Suddenly this trip has become much more bearable."

"Ha-ha," said Beldegard without a trace of humor.

"So, Liam, do you still want to move to a different camping site?" Annie asked.

Liam shook his head. "No need," he said, and patted the sword at his hip. "If that monster shows up again, I can take care of it."

CHAPTER 4

IT TOOK MOST OF THE NEXT MORNING to search the perimeter of the lake for signs of the dwarf. The day was getting hot when Beldegard snuffled the ground under a pine tree and finally announced he'd found a few footprints belonging to the little man. Liam inspected the prints carefully and declared they were at least two weeks old.

"Now what?" Annie asked the bear prince after they'd all agreed that the dwarf must not have been near the lake for days.

"Now we go visit the old widow who gave me shelter each winter. She lives about an hour away."

"Fine," said Annie, "but don't tell her who I am. People always act differently when they know."

"Why do we need to visit her anyway?" asked Liam.

Beldegard grunted and swung his heavy head toward Liam. "Because she may have seen him and it's as good a place to start as any." As he turned away and began to amble through the forest, he muttered, "I hate it when people question everything I do, but that's what I get for traveling with people like them."

Liam's brows drew together. "What do you mean, 'people like them'?"

"Royalty!" the bear prince snapped. "You people are so demanding. If you weren't royalty, you wouldn't ask so many questions."

Annie was already following Beldegard. Liam snorted as he stepped in line behind her and replied, "And if you explained yourself, we wouldn't have to ask questions at all."

❧

Their progress was slow as they walked single file through the forest, but eventually Beldegard led them to a little-traveled trail. After that they were able to move faster and it wasn't long before they entered a valley where the branches of the trees met overhead, and the air was cooler and sweeter smelling. The trail led them to a stream that wasn't much bigger than a trickle, yet someone had built a bridge from one side to the other. Just beyond the stream, a small cottage nestled among the trees. With a thatched roof that resembled a saggy straw hat and two small arched windows on either side of the front door, Annie thought it looked like a friendly, if slightly dopey, face.

Beldegard perked up when they saw the stream. Annie and Liam had to hurry to keep up with him as he trotted across the bridge and up to the front door of the cottage. They watched as he raised his huge front paw and tapped the door. "Mother Hubbard! It's me, Beldegard!" he called.

A moment later the door creaked open and a medium-size dog with curly brown fur bounded out of the cottage to bark and race around Beldegard, apparently not the least bit afraid. The bear prince stood stoically as the little creature jumped up to lick his face. When the dog ran back inside, Beldegard glanced at Annie and Liam. "The first time I knocked on this door it was winter. A mother and her two daughters were starving inside and that dog didn't even have a bone to gnaw. I brought them some game to feed them, and gave them a few gold coins in the spring. For the past two years, I've spent my winters in this cottage. Come inside and I'll introduce you."

Annie looked around as she stepped over the threshold. The cottage was a simple structure with two rooms below and a loft above. A table was shoved up against one wall of the main room while another wall boasted a small fireplace. Brightly colored cushions decorated with needlepoint flowers covered the seats of three wooden chairs set beside the table, while plumper cushions with needlepoint sayings rested on a bench beside the fireplace. Dried herbs strung together in bundles hung from the ceiling and Annie could smell meat roasting in the other room. Although it didn't appear to be a wealthy household, the cottage was cozy and inviting. The only thing that Annie thought was unusual was the mellow tune that declared the presence of a good kind of magic.

A gray-haired woman standing by the fireplace smiled and reached out her hand to Beldegard. She was a handsome woman with her hair pulled back from her face, showing off her high cheekbones and large, dark eyes. The bear prince padded toward her to bump her hand with his head. The woman's smile broadened. When Liam coughed, she glanced toward her other new guests and raised a questioning eyebrow.

"These are my friends," said Beldegard. "They're helping me with a quest."

"How nice," said a voice, and Annie turned to see another woman whom she hadn't really looked at yet. This woman had white hair and the pleasant round face of a sweet old grandmother. She was knitting in a rocking chair by the window while two orange-and-white kittens played by her feet.

Annie gasped and would have run from the cottage if Liam hadn't been standing in the way. It was Granny Bentbone, the witch who had invited children into her gingerbread cottage only to fatten them up for dinner. Although Annie knew who she was, the old woman didn't seem to recognize Annie. Granny Bentbone smiled and nodded, then went back to her knitting.

Annie swallowed hard. She had hoped that she'd never see Granny Bentbone again, and certainly wasn't expecting to find her here. Annie's heart was racing and her hands suddenly felt clammy. She tried to think about what she should do, until she realized that Mother Hubbard was talking again.

"...my cousin. Her house was destroyed in the storm we had a few days ago. I met her in the woods, and when she told me about her dilemma, I invited her to stay here with me. I've been so lonely ever since Snow White moved away and Rose Red started working at the Gasping Guppy Tavern."

Granny Bentbone was her cousin? Beldegard had said that Mother Hubbard was nice. Yes, she had magic, or at least there was some in the cottage, but she must not use it for anything bad or the music wouldn't sound so sweet. If she'd invited Granny Bentbone to live with her, she probably didn't have any idea what her cousin was capable of doing. Annie wanted to tell Mother Hubbard, but what if the woman didn't believe her? Not only did she not have any proof, Granny Bentbone didn't look as if she could hurt a mosquito, let alone a child.

"Do you plan to stay the night?" Mother Hubbard asked Beldegard.

"We don't have time," said Beldegard. "I came to ask

if you'd seen the dwarf I was hunting. You know—the one who turned me into a bear."

"Do I know you?" Granny Bentbone asked.

Annie turned back to the old woman and gulped. Granny Bentbone was staring at her, tapping her chin with one finger. She no longer looked quite so pleasant or friendly.

"I don't think so," said Annie. She'd been disguised as a boy and calling herself Charlie when she met the old woman before. Too bad she was dressed as a boy again.

"No, I've never seen your dwarf," Mother Hubbard told Beldegard. Her smile faded as she faced the bear prince and Annie thought she saw the first sign of uncertainty in the woman's eyes. Mother Hubbard took a step back, bumping into the dog, who was sitting behind her. His body was perfectly still, although it had been quivering with excitement just moments before. His ears were back now too, and he was staring at Beldegard as if he were seeing the bear prince for the first time.

"You look so familiar …," Granny Bentbone said to Annie, leaning forward in the rocker.

During their last encounter, she'd learned that the old woman had a terrible memory, but now and then she could remember things very clearly. If Granny Bentbone remembered that Annie had destroyed her house, no one would believe it was because she'd been trying to force Annie into the room where she locked children in cages.

Everyone turned to the dog when he began to growl. His ears were pinned back and his fur was bristling when he took a tentative step toward Beldegard.

Mother Hubbard scowled, then turned suddenly and took a step toward the bench. Annie was surprised when the woman picked up one of the cushions, plumped it with her hands, and set it back down.

What an odd thing to do, thought Annie, *unless . . .*

Annie glanced at the cushion. PEACE, HARMONY, HAPPINESS read the needlepoint decoration. *So that's it!* Annie thought, noticing that the tune that she'd heard when she entered the cottage had faded. The cushion itself must have been the source of the magic, ensuring that anyone who entered the cottage would be peaceful and happy. Just like the music, the magic was fading because Annie was there. It was time for her to leave.

"I think I'll wait outside," she said as she scurried around Liam and out the door.

Annie had just crossed the threshold when she heard the sound of running feet and caught a glimpse of a figure darting into the underbrush at the edge of the woods. Branches shook wildly, then stopped suddenly as if the runner had decided to hide instead of run. Curious, Annie walked to the grass that the figure had crossed and bent down to see if he had left footprints.

She saw two distinct ones; the tracks were about the size of Annie's own feet, and led back to the cottage. Still bent over, Annie followed them. Whoever had made the tracks had been standing at the window and could have witnessed everything that went on inside.

"Annie!" Liam called as he stepped out of the cottage. "We're going into the village."

"Shh!" she said, gesturing for him to come closer.

"Mother Hubbard remembered something. It seems Rose Red told her that someone came into the Gasping Guppy asking about the dwarf," said Beldegard as he followed Liam out the door. "She suggested we go talk to Rosey."

"Would you please be quiet?" Annie whispered. "Someone has been spying on us and is hiding in those bushes." When she pointed at the underbrush, she could have sworn she saw them quiver.

Liam nodded. Pointing at himself, he gestured at a spot on the other side of the underbrush. When Annie nodded back, he slipped away, walking so quietly that she couldn't hear him.

"I think I'll go look for some berries," Beldegard announced in a loud voice, shambling around the shrubs from the other direction.

Annie was watching the shrubs, waiting for one of her companions to do something, when the branches thrashed and a slim person in the clothes of a stable

boy burst free. In a flash, Annie darted after the fleeing figure and threw herself onto his back, knocking
him to the ground.

"Ow! Get off me!" the figure cried. Startled, Annie
grabbed his shoulder and flipped him over, only to see
her sister, Gwendolyn, glaring up at her.

"What are you doing here?" Annie demanded.

"Let me up and I'll tell you," Gwendolyn said, tucking her hair back in the boy's cap she was wearing.

"Oh, for . . . ," Annie muttered as she got to her feet,
and thrust out her hand to help her sister up. "How
long have you been following us?" she asked, annoyed.

Gwendolyn stood and brushed off her clothes. "Since
just after you left. I crossed the drawbridge the moment
you entered the forest."

"But I saw you on the parapet waving that stupid
handkerchief at Beldegard!" said Annie.

"That was one of my ladies-in-waiting. I'd already
changed my clothes and was waiting until you couldn't
see me. I'm surprised it took you so long to notice that I
was following you. I expected you to spot me long before
this. Beldegard!" she called as the bear prince emerged
from the underbrush covered in bits of twigs and leaves.
"Here I am, my love! I've come to join you on your quest!"

"I *should* make you go home," Annie grumbled.

"But you won't—not by myself," Gwendolyn told her.
"You knew I wanted to come with you! Now you can't
do anything about it. I'm going, no matter what you say."

CHAPTER 5

ANNIE SIGHED. She had hoped that Liam and Beldegard would agree with her and want to send Gwendolyn home, but Liam had said that someone would have to go with her and he wasn't about to go, and Beldegard didn't see any reason why she couldn't join them. Now Annie was stuck traveling with her sister, who would make demands, expect to get her own way, and probably be as useless as a horse in a row boat. Life wasn't fair.

Once again Beldegard took the lead, only this time Gwendolyn was beside him. Annie and Liam were walking far enough back that they were able to hold their own private conversation.

"What happened at that cottage?" Liam asked. "One minute everyone seemed friendly and the next minute you could cut the tension with a dull sword."

"There was a needlepoint cushion that said 'harmony, happiness, and peace,' or something like that. I heard the magic as soon as we walked in. Someone had imbued the cushion with magic so that everyone in the cottage would be nice and get along."

"You mean they filled a cushion with friendly magic?"

"Exactly. An object can be used to do something magical, but my presence caused the magic to go away. I read about it in a book just the other day. Ever since people started asking me to undo their magic, I've been looking through all the books on magic I can find so I know what I might come across."

"Huh," said Liam. "A magic cushion would explain why Mother Hubbard would let a bear into her house in the first place. She expected him to behave himself because of the magic."

Annie nodded. "And I'm sure it worked just fine until I made the magic fade."

"So what about that other old woman? She said she recognized you. Had you ever seen her before?"

"Unfortunately, yes. She's the horrible witch I told you about who feeds children to fatten them up so she can eat them."

"That was *her*! I wish I'd known," Liam said, suddenly looking serious. "I would have taken care of the old witch then and there."

"With her cousin standing by? For all we know, Mother Hubbard may be a witch herself. Just because she has a magic object that works on its own doesn't mean she wasn't the one who put the magic in it. And even if she is a good witch, we'd need proof before we can do anything about Granny Bentbone. No, what we need to do is get word to my father. He can send men to search what's left of the gingerbread cottage. The cages are probably still intact, and there were all those old children's clothes and toys in the loft. If the men dig through the rubble, they might be able to find something. Once they have proof, they can deal with the nasty old witch."

"Good idea," said Liam. "I'll send word from the village. If we're lucky, we'll find the dwarf and be back in time to help your father's men."

Annie shuddered. "I wouldn't call that lucky. I'd be a whole lot happier if I never saw that old woman again."

⁊

Set on the shore of the Crystal River, the village of Farley's Crossing was a good-sized village built at the only ferry crossing for miles around. Annie was eager to reach the tavern and sit down for a while, but Beldegard called for a halt just inside the tree line before they ever set foot in the village.

"I've been here before, back when I was still human. It's a nice enough place, but the people here wouldn't take too kindly to a bear walking through the center of their village. The tavern is on the main street. You three get some supper and I'll meet you at the back of the tavern. Find Rosey and tell her that I'm out back and want to talk to her."

"I'll stay with you, my love," said Gwendolyn. "I'm not dressed to go to such a public place."

The princess glanced down at the boy's clothes she was wearing and plucked at a sleeve with distaste. For once Annie agreed with her sister's decision. Gwendolyn might be dressed as a stable boy, but she still had the face and figure of a beautiful princess. If anyone got a good look at her, she was bound to draw attention of a different sort. It didn't matter if Annie was dressed as a girl or a boy because people rarely spared her a second glance.

"Liam and I will take care of this," said Annie. "We'll bring you something to eat."

The main street ran straight to the dock where the ferry waited to take on passengers and cargo. The street was lined with shops and cottages, most in good repair. While Liam found someone to take a message about Granny Bentbone to King Halbert, Annie studied the buildings, but didn't see anything big enough to house a tavern until she reached the river's edge. An old building to the left of the dock had a sign over the front door that read FERRY. Chickens scratched the ground for insects just outside the door and Annie spotted clothes drying on a sagging rope behind the back of the building. Apparently the building was the ferryman's home as well as his place of business.

Across the street on the other side of the dock was another, newer building. The sign hanging over the door read THE GASPING GUPPY with a picture of a small fish, its mouth wide open as it gasped for air. Liam joined Annie as she approached the tavern. They had to step out of the way when a party of travelers arrived and swung down off their horses, handing the reins to boys who came running from the stable next door.

"I hope no one recognizes me here," said Annie. "We're still close enough to home that they might know my reputation. Helping people with their magic problems is just as bad as having them hurry away when I show up."

"I wouldn't worry about it," Liam told her, cupping her elbow with his hand to guide her to the door. "No one is going to expect to see royalty here, and we both blend in better than most princes and princesses would."

"Which one is Rose Red?" Annie said, peering into the darkened room where three tavern maids scurried from table to table.

"I didn't think to ask Beldegard what she looked like, so I guess we'll just have to ask in here," said Liam. "Why don't we sit down and get something to eat? I don't know about you, but I'd enjoy a nice hot meal."

Although it was still early in the day, there weren't

many empty seats in the room. Liam finally found two by the back wall hidden from view behind a large man who spoke in a loud, boisterous voice. Once they took their seats, Annie was afraid that the tavern maids wouldn't know they were there, but they'd been sitting at the table for only a few minutes when a man announced that the ferry was about to leave and most of the people in the room stood up. Annie was glad that the big man and his smaller companion were among them; the man's booming voice was getting on her nerves.

When everyone who was riding on the ferry had gone, there were only half a dozen people left in the room, including Annie and Liam. A tavern maid with long salt-and-pepper hair spotted them right away and came plodding over. "What can I get you?" she asked Liam.

"Is your name Rose Red?" Liam replied.

"Rosey!" the woman called to a dark-haired girl about Annie's age bending over another table. "This gentleman is asking for you."

As the older tavern maid walked off, Rose Red glanced at them and went back to talking to the man at the other table. A few minutes later she laughed at something he'd said, gave him a pat on his cheek, and sashayed to where Annie and Liam were waiting.

"You asked for me?" she said, eyeing Liam in an appreciative way.

"I did if you're Rose Red," he replied. "What are you serving tonight?"

"Fish stew," she replied as she continued to look him over. "It's what we serve every day."

"Two bowls please, and some bread and cooked fish for the road."

"Coming right up," she said, and turned away without giving Annie a glance.

"She didn't ask what I wanted," said Annie. "For all she knows, you might be really hungry and want all of that for yourself."

Liam smiled. "Don't worry, I'll share it with you." He reached across the table to take her hand, saying, "I like when it's just the two of us the way it was when we traveled through the kingdoms, looking for princes for Gwendolyn. That was the most fun I've ever had."

"I thought so, too," said Annie, "or at least I would have if I hadn't been so worried that we might not find the right prince. I don't know what I would have done if Gwennie hadn't woken up."

"I would have helped you look until we found the right one. You know I wouldn't have left you on your own. You mean too much to me. You've been my princess since the day I took the guard's oath to protect you and your family from my mother and brother. But now I feel as if—"

Annie and Liam turned their heads when a chair banged into a wall. Two middle-aged men sitting at a table by the door had been gobbling their food as if they were starving. One had gotten to his feet so suddenly that he'd knocked his chair over. He was fumbling through his pocket when his companion slapped a coin on the table. Gathering their satchels, they scurried from the room.

"They'll have to hurry if they want to catch the ferry," said a voice from a table near Annie and Liam.

Annie glanced at the young man sitting there. He was attractive enough to turn the head of any girl, which would have made Annie suspect magic if he hadn't been so obviously poor. Dressed in the clothes of a farm worker, his hands were callused and rough and the soles of his boots were thin from walking many miles. What was unusual about him, however, was that his companion was a large gray cat, sitting on the chair across from him, wearing boots of fine-tooled leather.

"I told you we need to practice," the cat whispered to the young man. "Now's as good a time as any."

"But do we have to do it here?" the young man whispered back.

"Why not?" whispered the cat. "These simple folk will believe anything. Just follow my lead like I told you before. Good day," said the cat, turning to face Annie and Liam. "Let me introduce myself. I am Puss, and this is the Marquis of Carabas."

"That's nice," said Annie. She glanced at Liam, who smiled at her and winked.

"Indeed!" said the cat. "He is a very important person who is wealthy and owns much land."

Liam leaned forward in his seat. "Where is Carabas located? I'm afraid I've never heard of it."

"Ah, that is because it is far from here, located in the kingdom of Dorinocco," said Puss.

Liam snorted and covered it with a pretend cough. Annie couldn't help but smile. He was the second son of the king and queen of Dorinocco, and had been made the crown prince when his brother was banished for nearly starting a war with Treecrest. If anyone would know about the towns in Dorinocco, it would be Liam.

"How interesting," said Liam. "You see, I've traveled extensively throughout Dorinocco, yet I've never heard of Carabas."

"Well, it's there," the young man said, sounding belligerent.

"And what brings you to Treecrest?" asked Annie.

"We have heard that the princess of Treecrest is finally free of her curse," Puss hurried to say. "As the most beautiful princess in the world, she will make the ideal bride for the Marquis."

"We're on our way there so I can win her heart," said the young man.

Annie struggled not to laugh. "I've heard that she's already taken."

"Really?" squeaked the Marquis, making Annie wonder just how old he was if his voice was still changing.

"About Carabas...," Liam began.

"It is time for us to go," the cat said to the young man.

"It was nice meeting you," the Marquis told Annie and Liam.

"Now!" said the cat as he jumped off his chair.

Rose Red appeared in the door, carrying two steaming bowls of stew, and had to step aside as the young man and his cat hurried past. "I'm glad I had them pay before I brought their supper," she said, setting the bowls on Annie and Liam's table. "That cat looked shifty to me. So, are you staying for a while or are you waiting for the next trip across on the ferry?" she asked Liam, still acting as if Annie weren't there.

"Actually," said Liam, "we came to talk to you. Or at least a friend of ours did. You do remember Beldegard, don't you?"

"Beldegard?" she said, looking puzzled. "I don't know any man by that name."

"He isn't a man exactly," Annie said. "He's a bear who used to be a man. A prince really, but then you probably know that."

Rose Red's eyes widened. "I know he used to say he was a prince, but he really is? Ah, well, that's neither here nor there. What good is he if he's still just a bear?"

"We're on a quest to get him turned back," Liam told her. "If all goes well, he won't be a bear for much longer."

"And he's here, you say?" said Rose Red with a spark in her eye.

Liam nodded. "We'll take you to him as soon as you bring us that cooked fish and bread we asked for. He's hungry, too."

"I'll be right back," said Rose Red, and hurried from the room.

"I think she's eager to see him," Liam said.

"Indeed," replied Annie. "Now that she knows he really is a prince and has a chance of becoming a man again. We'd better eat fast. I don't think she'll want to wait for us to finish."

❧

"Beldegard!" Rose Red exclaimed as if he were the most important person in the world. With a cry of delight, she ran to the bear and hugged him, shoving Gwendolyn out of the way.

"Pardon me!" said the princess, but Rose Red kept hugging the bear prince, who didn't seem to mind.

"I wish you'd greet me like that," Liam whispered to Annie.

"Get turned into a bear and I will," she murmured back.

"Beldegard!" Gwendolyn wailed when it looked as if Rose Red would never let go.

The bear prince grunted. "Uh, you're making it hard for me to breathe," he told Rose Red, who dropped her arms and stepped aside to look at him.

"I'm so glad you came to see me, Beldy," she told him. "I've missed you so much. Why did you ever leave me?"

"Beldy?" said Gwendolyn. "She actually calls you that?"

Beldegard sat up a little straighter. "You got a boy-friend, remember?"

"But Yardley ran off without a word!" Rose Red cried. "Can you imagine? And after he was gone I realized how much I loved you and I didn't know how to find you."

"He's been busy," Gwendolyn snapped at her. "Tell her why we're here," she said to Beldegard.

"Oh, right. We're looking for the dwarf who turned me into a bear. You remember, I told you all about him." Beldegard sighed when Rose Red gave him a blank look. "Short man, long white beard, leaf footprints, voice like a choked frog..."

"Sorry, I've never seen anyone like that," Rose Red said, shaking her head.

Thunder rumbled in the distance. Annie looked up to see dark clouds scudding overhead. "Your mother said you told her that someone came to the tavern asking about him," said Annie, turning back to Rose Red.

"Oh, *that* dwarf! Just a few days ago an old dwarf came in looking for his brother. He said there was a family emergency and his brother needed to come home. It had something to do with their grandfather being sick."

Annie turned her head when she heard someone whistling. A stable boy strode around the back of the building. He glanced at the group of people, stopping suddenly when he saw the bear. Turning on his heel, the boy ran back around the stable.

"I think I should go now," said Beldegard. "People around here are more likely to hunt bears than talk to them."

"Did the old dwarf mention where he came from?" Liam asked Rose Red.

"I'm not sure," she said, looking thoughtful. "He did say that he had come a long way. Oh, wait! I remember now! He said he was from the Dark Woods. Yes, that was it, I'm sure of it."

"There it is!" shouted the stable boy to the group of men following him. "See—it isn't on a chain. It's a wild bear, just like I told you!"

"I have to go!" said Beldegard. "We need to cross the river. Take the first ferry across and I'll meet you on the other side."

"But Beldegard!" Gwendolyn cried as the bear prince loped off.

"Don't forget me, Beldy!" cried Rose Red. "You know I always liked you better than I liked anyone else!"

"Out of the way!" a rough-looking man shouted at

Annie and the others as the mob armed with pitch-forks and grappling hooks tore after the bear prince.

"I hope he'll be all right!" Gwendolyn wailed, wringing her hands.

"He'll be fine," said Annie. "He's as smart as a human and as strong as a bear. I'm sure he'll figure something out."

CHAPTER 6

WHEN TEARS POOLED IN GWENDOLYN'S EYES, Annie patted her on her back. After years of being told to keep her distance from her parents and sister, she still wasn't comfortable touching them. "Don't worry," she said. "You'll see Beldegard again in a little while."

"No, she won't," said Rose Red, brushing the loose bear fur off her gown. "That was the last ferry for the day. The next one won't be leaving until morning."

"In that case I should look for a place we can spend the night," said Liam. "Do you know where we can find a room?" he asked Rose Red.

She nodded and pointed at the tavern. "There are a couple of rooms upstairs, but they go fast. People spend the night so they can board the first ferry in the morning."

"I'll see what I can get," said Liam. "Wait here, ladies. I'll be right back."

As Liam hurried off, Rose Red eyed Gwendolyn. "So, you think you're in love with the bear?" she asked, flipping her hair over her shoulder.

"I *am* in love with him. He's my one true love!"

"Yeah, right. And I'm a royal princess."

"I'll have you know that I *am*—"

"Not going to wait here any longer," interrupted Annie. "Come on, Gwennie."

"So why are you two wearing boys' clothes?" Rose Red said as she followed them to the tavern. "It's pretty obvious that you're girls—especially you," she said, looking Gwendolyn up and down.

"We…fell in the river and our clothes were ruined," Annie hurried to say before her sister could answer. She didn't want to people to know that they were princesses traveling in disguise with a prince and a bear as their escorts. Traveling was dangerous enough without drawing the attention of everyone on the road.

"There you are," said Liam. "I was just coming to get you. They had only one room left, so we're going to have to share."

Gwendolyn's eyes grew wide and she'd begun to shake her head when Annie grabbed her hand and tugged her toward the stairs. "That will do just fine," Annie said.

Rain was tapping at the window, letting only a grayish light through the wavery glass when Annie, Liam, and Gwendolyn stepped inside the small room. A bed just big enough for two nearly filled the area, leaving space for a tiny wash stand and one straight-backed chair by the door. Once everyone was inside, the room felt cramped and crowded. While Gwendolyn stood with her arms crossed, as if she didn't want to touch anything, Annie pulled back the covers to check the bed and Liam inspected the lock on the door.

"It's small, but it's clean," Annie said, sitting on the edge of the bed.

"And there's a good, sturdy lock," said Liam.

"I don't know what you two are thinking, but this just won't do!" Gwendolyn exclaimed.

"Shh! The walls are probably thin," Liam told her in a quiet voice. "We should keep our voices down if we don't want everyone to hear us."

"And we don't want people to know who we are," Annie added.

Gwendolyn looked confused. "Why not?"

Annie sighed. She knew her sister had never been out of the castle before, but even she had to know that the world was very different beyond the castle walls. "Because not everyone is nice out here," she told Gwendolyn.

"That's right," said Liam. "There are a lot of good

people in the world, but there are also a lot who would steal the shoes off your feet if given the chance."

Gwendolyn looked even more confused.

"He means you can't trust anyone you don't know," Annie told her. "Don't tell them who we are, or where we're going, or why. Understand?"

"I guess so," said Gwendolyn. "But I still don't think we should be sharing a room."

"Why?" asked Annie. "Because we're princesses, or because then I'd be close to you, or because Liam is a boy?"

Gwendolyn hesitated, making Annie wonder if her sister didn't consider all of the reasons valid.

"I could sleep outside," Liam offered, glancing at the door.

Annie shook her head. "Not in the rain. Gwennie and I can sleep on the bed and you can sleep on the floor."

"But, Annie!" said Gwendolyn. "You know what being near you does to me. I can't spend the whole night beside you!"

"Well, I'm not sleeping on the floor just so you can have a bed all to yourself!" Annie snapped. "If you want to sleep on the floor, be my guest!" She had spent her entire life trying to accommodate her sister, who wasn't even supposed to be here!

Gwendolyn dropped her gaze to the floor and said in a near whisper, "I suppose it doesn't matter. No one will see me in here, except you two."

"And that reminds me," said Annie, trying not to notice the look of desperation on her sister's face. "Rose Red was right. You really can't pass as a boy looking like that. We have to do something about your clothes."

"I have an extra shirt she can wear tomorrow," said Liam. "It's baggier than the one she has on." Setting his sack on the floor, he squatted down beside it and pulled out a clean, white shirt that would be huge on Gwendolyn.

The princess wrinkled her nose when he handed her the shirt. "I can't wear this!" she said, trying to hand it back to him. "It smells like fish!"

"Oh, yes. I forgot," said Liam, reaching into the bag again. "Here's your dinner. We got enough for you and Beldegard."

Gwendolyn dropped the shirt on the bed and sat as far from Annie as she could get. Annie half expected her to turn down the fish, knowing how picky her sister could be about the food she'd accept on her own silver plate at home, but she seemed so grateful when she took the greasy paper from Liam and opened it to see the succulent fish inside that Annie felt guilty for forgetting that her sister hadn't eaten.

Using her long, slender fingers, Gwendolyn broke off a morsel of fish and placed it on her tongue. The look of bliss on her face was so profound that Annie had to smile. Her smile grew even broader when Liam pulled another paper packet from his bag and said, "You and I might as well eat this, Annie. We didn't get to finish our stew and there's no use saving Beldegard's share. He'll have to fend for himself tonight anyway."

"I don't even know if a bear would eat cooked fish," Annie said. "And it might not be any good by tomorrow."

Moments later, the only sound to be heard in the little room was the patter of rain on the window.

℘

Annie woke, shaking, certain that something was in the room with her. She pinched her upper arm to make sure that she was awake. The tiny pain told her that she was, but even so, she could still hear a deep even breathing that meant she wasn't really alone. And then Liam rolled over on the floor beside the bed and Annie remembered where she was and who was with her.

The rain had stopped and it was late enough that the tavern had grown quiet for the last few hours before dawn. Annie lay on her back, staring at the ceiling as she waited for her racing heart to calm to a steadier beat. When she was no longer afraid that something was going to jump at her from the dark, she sat up to peek over the pillow that Gwennie had put between them. She could just make out her sister's shape under the blanket on the edge of the bed as far from Annie as she could manage. Before lying down again, she leaned over the other side of the bed and peered down at

Liam, tangled in his blanket with his head pillowed on his arms.

Moving as quietly as she could so as not to wake Gwendolyn, Annie slipped from the bed, took the blanket she had brought with her from her knapsack, and used it to cover Liam. He seemed so sweet and vulnerable that she couldn't resist bending down to kiss his cheek. The rain started again before she was back under the covers, the first taps on the glass sounding like insects trying to come in. By the time she closed her eyes, the rain's steady drumming was enough to lull her back to sleep.

༂

Annie woke the next morning to find someone she'd never seen before sleeping beside her. She knew right away that it was Gwendolyn, of course, and she knew she shouldn't be surprised. After all, Annie's lack of magic had had all night to undo the effects of Gwendolyn's magical gifts. But her sister looked so different that Annie couldn't stop staring.

Gwendolyn's hair was no longer buttercup blond. It was brown now, and would have been the same shade as her own if Annie's hadn't been sun-bleached from being outside so much. Her nose could no longer be called perfect, and her skin was no longer flawless, with a mole on her neck and a few freckles on her nose. Gwendolyn looked a lot like Annie, only older. For the first time in her life, Annie felt a special kind of kinship to the girl so many people considered the most beautiful princess in all the kingdoms.

Annie glanced at the floor beside the bed, but Liam had already folded the blankets and left the room. "Wake up," Annie said, turning back to Gwendolyn. "I'm going to get dressed and go find Liam."

"Huh?" mumbled her sister. "What did you—ahh!" she shrieked, staring at a fistful of her own hair. "What happened to me?"

"Lower your voice!" said Annie. "You know perfectly well what happened to you." A surge of the familiar resentment washed over her, dousing the warm feeling that had begun just moments before. "Don't worry, I'll leave and you'll go back to looking like your gorgeous self in minutes."

Although getting dressed meant nothing more than running her fingers through her hair, covering it with the cap again, and slipping her feet into her shoes, it seemed to take too long with Gwendolyn watching her. Annie was almost out the door when she noticed Liam's shirt. Snatching it off the chair, she tossed it at her sister, saying, "You're supposed to wear this today, remember?"

"Wait, Annie!" Gwendolyn said. "I'm sorry."

"Sorry for what?"

"For acting like you're some kind of monster that I

have to keep at bay. I know you never meant to make me look less beautiful, and I was always telling you to stay away, but if you had made my beauty fade it really wouldn't have been your fault. Although actually it would have been, I mean, it was last night, but, well, you know what I mean, don't you?"

"I suppose I do," Annie said, surprised that her sister was even attempting to apologize. "And it's all right. You were doing what you thought you had to do. Listen, I'll meet you downstairs. Don't take too long. We don't know when that ferry will be leaving."

Annie was halfway down the stairs when the door to the chamber flew open and Gwendolyn darted out, still stuffing her hair inside her cap. The sisters gave each other tentative smiles, then came down the stairs together. Reaching the hallway that led into the main room of the tavern, they found Liam talking to the owner.

Liam nodded when he saw them. "Good, I'm glad you're up. The ferry is leaving in half an hour. Here, take these," he said, opening a small brown sack. "I've been awake for hours. While you two slept I explored the village and found a bakery on Drury Lane that makes great muffins."

Annie was reaching for the muffin when she noticed that the tavern owner was staring at Gwendolyn with his mouth hanging open. It was an expression Annie was used to seeing people wearing when she was around her sister; she just hadn't expected to see it now. When she glanced at Gwennie, she saw that that wisp of hair that peeked out from under her cap was already blond, her nose was back to normal, and her skin was nearly flawless.

"Let's eat these outside," Annie said, taking Gwendolyn by the hand.

"Let go," Gwendolyn said once they were walking down the street toward the ferry. "I need both hands to eat this."

Annie shook her head. "I'm not letting go until we're on that ferry, and maybe not even then." She noticed with satisfaction that Gwendolyn was already looking a little less beautiful. "We're going to have to think of something to disguise her," she said to Liam. "The shirt helps, but it's not enough. Maybe we could plaster her face with mud."

"Don't you dare!" exclaimed Gwendolyn.

"We could wrap her head in bandages," Liam suggested.

"You will not!" Gwendolyn cried.

"Then I guess you're just going to have to stick close to me until we get away from all these people," Annie told her, gesturing to the small crowd already gathering by the ferry.

"And even that might not be enough," Liam said under his breath as two young men turned and gave

Gwendolyn appreciative looks. Setting his hand on his sword, he herded the sisters toward the other side of the dock where they waited, huddled together, while he went to speak to the ferryman.

"Have any dwarves ridden on your ferry lately?" Liam asked the man.

The old man took a licorice root out of his mouth long enough to say, "Maybe."

"Two males? One was older than the other?"

"Maybe," said the man.

"Would this help loosen your tongue?" Liam asked, showing the man a coin.

The man's mouth widened into a grin. "That it would," he said, snatching the coin from Liam's hand. "Two dwarves rode my ferry less than a week ago. They argued the whole way across. Seems they hadn't seen each other in a while. From the things they said to each other, I think they were brothers and the younger one was the black sheep of the family. He was surly and unfriendly. I was glad when he got off my boat. The older one was all right, though. I didn't mind him."

"Did they say where they were going?" asked Liam.

"Nope," the old man said, tucking the coin in his leather pouch. "I didn't ask them either. But they headed north when they reached the road."

When the ferryman left to start loading horses and cargo, Liam found his way back to the girls.

"Did you learn anything about the dwarf?" asked Annie.

"Just that he's unpleasant and isn't getting along with his brother," Liam replied. "They did go this way, though, so we're headed the right way."

❧

After the storm of the night before, the trip across the river was rough, with whitecaps slapping the ferry so that water ran over the sides, drenching shoes and hems. People were too busy trying to calm their horses and keep their footing to pay much attention to each other, but Annie noticed that the young men looked in Gwennie's direction the moment they set foot on dry land. She was glad she had kept hold of her sister's elbow the entire trip when the young men turned away, no longer interested.

Before the other travelers had gathered their horses and started out, Gwendolyn was already studying the forest on either side of the road, looking for Beldegard, while Liam wandered off, his eyes on the ground. Annie was about to ask him what he was doing when he called her over and pointed at a small footprint with a leaf design in the center. "Now we know for sure that we're following the right dwarf," he told her.

The ferryman kept casting odd looks at Annie and her companions, so they finally walked down the road until they were out of sight of the river. They hadn't gone far when they heard crashing in the forest and Beldegard bounded out, his mouth split in a huge grin.

"It's about time!" he said, nudging Gwendolyn even as she bent down to kiss his furry head.

"I'm sorry it took us so long, dear one," said Gwendolyn, "but we had to wait for the next ferry trip over."

"Now what?" asked Liam. "You said we had to cross the river, and here we are."

Beldegard began to walk with Gwendolyn by his side. "According to Rose Red, the dwarf claimed to be from the Dark Woods," he said over his shoulder. "I know of no Dark Woods, but there is a Dark Forest in Dorinocco, and it looks like the dwarf is headed there."

"And if we don't find him in this Dark Forest?" Liam called as he waited for Annie to join him.

"Then we keep looking until we do find him," the bear prince replied, then turned his head to talk to Gwendolyn.

Liam was scowling when Annie began to walk with him. "We should set a time limit on this expedition," he said.

"Why don't we give it a week?" asked Annie.

"I was thinking more like a few days," said Liam, his mouth set in a grim line.

CHAPTER 7

ANNIE PLUCKED A CHUNK OF CHEESE off the tip of Liam's knife. They had been walking all morning and had stopped to share the food that he had bought in the village. Beldegard had already wandered off to forage on his own. "I've been thinking," Annie told her companions. "We really need to find the dwarf and change Beldegard back as soon as we can, and not just so we can go home. Now that word has gotten out that the curse can no longer hurt Gwennie, all sorts of crazies are going to show up at the castle wanting to marry her. With an entire kingdom at stake, they won't care if she's found her true love as long as she isn't actually married."

"Crazies?" asked Liam.

Annie nodded. "Like that boy and his cat that were on their way to the castle to win her hand."

"What boy?" Gwendolyn asked, a piece of bread halfway to her mouth.

"We met him when we went into the tavern to find Rose Red," said Liam. "He had a talking cat with him who claimed the boy was a wealthy noble named the Marquis of Carabas, but the boy's shoes were worn and he had the calluses of a farmer. It was obvious they were going to try to pull some sort of scam. They couldn't even tell me where Carabas was located."

"And this boy wanted to marry me?" asked Gwendolyn.

"That's what he told us," said Annie. "And you know he's bound to be just one of many."

Gwendolyn shrugged. "They'll leave me alone once they hear about Beldegard."

"Not necessarily," said Annie. "Beldegard is still a bear and you aren't married to him yet. People won't believe you're taken until he's turned back into a man and you two are officially wed."

"Then I guess I'm glad I came with you," Gwendolyn said, giving her sister her brightest smile. "If I were at home now, I'd have to fend them off by myself."

"Shh!" said Liam. "I hear someone coming this way."

Annie turned to Liam, but he shook his head and put his finger to his lips. A moment later she heard a clear sweet voice whistling. And then a figure in a red cape appeared among the trees. Although a hood was covering the person's face, Annie could tell from her long skirts that it was a girl.

"She's getting close," Annie whispered. "Maybe we should make some noise so we don't startle her." Liam stood up and pretend-coughed. "Or we could do that," Annie murmured as the hood veered so that it was coming straight toward them.

The girl had almost reached them when she pushed the hood back from her face. She couldn't have been more then ten or eleven years old, with dark brown hair and a sunny smile. "Hello," she said, setting her basket on the ground so she could curtsy.

Gwendolyn glanced at the girl and nodded.

"Good day," said Annie. "We're looking for the Dark Forest. Do you know if we're getting close?"

"Oh, yes! It's not far now. I'm going that way to visit my granny. My mother sends her food and gossip from the village and I get to share both with Granny. I visit her every week, although I went just yesterday and she was sick, so I'm going back today with more food. I'm happy to do it because it gets me out of the house for a day and I don't have to take care of my younger brothers and sisters. I have seven brothers and three sisters and I'm the oldest of the girls."

"We should get going," said Liam.

The girl clapped her hands and grinned. "If you're going to the Dark Forest, too, we should go together! I never have company on my walks."

When Liam grumbled and started walking, the girl skipped ahead to join him. "My name is Gloria, but most people call me Little Red Riding Hood. My granny made this cape for me because she said I should wear something red when I'm in the forest. There are lots of hunters and not all of them are as careful as they should be, but they won't shoot me when they see my red cape."

"I see," Liam said, and Annie had to grin.

"Why are you smiling?" demanded Gwendolyn, falling into step beside Annie. "Beldegard probably won't join us as long as that girl is here. He's gotten very sensitive about people's reactions to him ever since those men chased him off. Why are we going with the girl anyway? Beldegard knows how to find the Dark Forest. We really don't need her help."

"I know," said Annie. "But there's no real harm if we're going in the same direction. I'm sure Beldegard will be able to find us. So tell me, what do you think of Gloria's cape? I noticed that we couldn't see her face very well when she had her hood up."

Gwendolyn glanced at the girl and shrugged. "I guess so."

"It might even be more concealing than mud or bandages," Annie continued.

"What are you talking about?" asked Gwendolyn. "I don't . . . Oh! I see what you mean. Do you suppose she would sell it to me? It is small, though."

Annie shrugged. "It wouldn't hurt to ask. Although I

was hoping we could ask her granny to make you one. The color red does draw attention. Maybe a more subtle color would be better."

Gwendolyn's expression brightened. "Pink, perhaps!"

"Or brown."

"Or fuchsia!"

"This is not going to be easy," Annie muttered to herself.

❧

They had walked only a short distance farther when the oaks, maples, and elms gave way to fir trees growing in ragged rows. The trees grew taller as they continued on, casting deep shadows beneath their branches. Annie loved the smell of the needles and took a deep breath even as she noticed how dark it had become.

"I guess this is the Dark Forest," said Gwendolyn.

Annie nodded. "That's a good name for it. I wonder where—"

"Here we are!" Gloria sang out as they reached the edge of a small clearing. Swinging the basket from her arm, she skipped ahead to rap on the wooden door of a sweet little cottage with ivy climbing its sturdy stone walls. A cat peeked at them from among the ferns growing at the corner of the cottage while another strode past, its tail in the air. "Granny, it's me!" the girl called.

A curtain twitched aside and a face peered out for an instant before the curtain fell back in place.

"You're not going in, are you?" Gwendolyn asked Annie. "Because if you are, I think I'll stay out here and wait for Beldegard."

Little Red Riding Hood had raised her hand to knock again when a creaky voice called out, "Come in, dearie!"

Annie glanced at Liam as the girl opened the door and stepped inside. "Did you see that?" Annie asked him.

"I sure did," said Liam. "Either that girl has the ugliest granny I've ever seen, or something isn't right here."

"What? Did I miss something?" asked Gwendolyn. "Do you hear magic, Annie?"

Annie shook her head. "It's not that," she said, and followed Liam into the cottage.

"Shut the door, dearie," said a creaky voice. "The bright light hurts my eyes."

Little Red Riding Hood brushed past Annie to shut the door, leaving them all in the near dark. Annie had taken only a few steps into the room when she tripped over something and fell against Liam. He grabbed her arm and held her until she had her feet under her, but even then something bumped into her legs and made her stagger.

As her eyes grew used to the dim light filtering through the closed curtains, Annie saw that the cottage was just one room. A large bed filled the center of the room and in the bed lay a figure in a nightgown and ruffled cap. Little Red Riding Hood was already standing by the end of the bed, holding the basket with both hands. "Look, Granny, I brought you visitors."

"How nice," her grandmother rasped. "And what did you bring me in your basket? Do I smell baked ham?" There was a loud sniffing sound, then Granny added, "And blueberry tarts!"

"Granny isn't feeling well," Little Red Riding Hood said, turning to Liam and Annie. "She has a wasting disease and needs lots of food to keep up her strength. She told me so yesterday."

"That's right, dearie. So why don't you just set that basket on the bed and I'll..."

"Ooh, Granny," the girl said, taking a step closer. "What big eyes you have."

"I know, I know! Didn't we go through this yesterday?" said Granny. "I have big eyes, the better to see you with, and big ears, the better to hear you with, and a big nose because it runs in the family. Now if you'll just—"

"Mworr!" A large cat jumped on the bed and padded across Granny's chest. "Get off me, stupid cat," the old woman said, pushing it aside.

"Granny, you must be really sick," said her granddaughter. "You usually let the cats walk all over you."

"How many cats do you have, Granny?" asked Annie.

Two cats emerged from the shadows and jumped onto the bed. One strode up to Granny and plumped down on her stomach, swiping its long tail across her face. The other sat on the edge of the bed and glared at her.

When the old woman hesitated, Little Red Riding Hood spoke up. "Granny has twenty-two cats, although the number changes all the time."

"That's right," Granny said, sounding as if she was speaking through gritted teeth. "I do love cats. Now, if you'll excuse me, I need my rest. Just leave the basket on the bed and I'll take care of putting the food away. Oh, and be sure to come back tomorrow, Granddaughter, dear. The delicious food you bring is making me feel much better."

Annie knew something was wrong, other than just the old woman's poor health, but she didn't know what to do to prove it. Maybe if she went outside, she and Liam could figure it out. "We're sorry we stopped by at such a bad time," she said. "I hope you're well soon. Liam and I will leave so you and Gloria can talk before you go back to sleep."

"Who's Gloria?" asked the old woman.

Annie scowled. Either the woman's memory was going, or it wasn't the grandmother at all. If Annie was wrong, the worst that could happen was she would embarrass herself. But if she was right...Keeping an eye on the figure in the bed, Annie stepped to the door and flung it wide. While Little Red Riding Hood and her grandmother cried out in protest, Annie went from window to window, dragging the curtains open, letting the tree-filtered sunlight in.

"It's a wolf!" Liam cried, dashing to the bed even as he drew his sword.

Little Red Riding Hood turned back to the bed. Seeing the long, furry face under her grandmother's ruffled cap, she cried out in horror.

With one motion, the wolf threw back the covers and leaped from the bed. Snatching the basket from Little Red Riding Hood's hands, it darted around Annie and Liam and out the door.

"What did you do with my granny!" Little Red Riding Hood shouted after the fleeing wolf.

"I thought this room smelled bad because she had so many cats," said Liam. "I never would have guessed it was a wolf."

"And a talking one at that," said Annie. "I've seen more talking animals in the last few days than I've seen in my entire lifetime before this."

"Gloria, are you all right?" a man asked, ducking to enter the cottage. He was a big man with the clothes of a huntsman and a face that was an older, male version of Little Red Riding Hood's.

With a strangled sob, Little Red Riding Hood flew into his arms and buried her face in his tunic. "Oh, Uncle Olaf, the wolf that pestered me yesterday was here, and I thought it was Granny, and Granny's gone and I think the wolf ate her."

"That wolf didn't eat your granny!" said the man. "It chased her out of her house yesterday and she came to mine. I was hunting and didn't get to talk to her until this morning, but then I came right over to see what was going on. The wolf didn't hurt you, did it?"

Little Red Riding Hood shook her head. "But it stole Mama's basket."

The big man laughed. "If that's all we have to worry about, we're fine. And who are these people, if I may ask?"

"Just travelers on our way, now that we know the little girl is all right," said Liam.

"More travelers!" said the huntsman. "I've never seen so many strangers passing through this part of the forest before. First I saw those two dwarves, and now you."

"Did you see them recently?" Liam asked, pausing at the threshold. "Was one older than the other?"

"Did you talk to them?" asked Annie. "What direction were they going?"

"It was one day last week," the huntsman replied. "I was checking my snares up by the ridge when I saw them from a distance. They seemed to be arguing, so I left them alone. They were headed north. And yes," he said, glancing at Liam. "They both had white hair, but one was stooped, so I assume he was older."

"At least we know they came this way," Liam told Annie as they stepped outside.

"Finally!" Gwennie declared. She was standing at the edge of the forest with her arms crossed, tapping her foot. "You were in there so long! I found Beldegard. He's waiting for us just up the trail. Did you remember to ask about the hood?"

"What hood?" asked Liam.

The door to the cottage opened and Little Red Riding Hood came running out. "Good," she cried when she saw them. "You haven't gone yet. I told Uncle Olaf that you were the ones who showed me that it was a wolf and not my grandmother in Granny's clothes. He said I should say thank you."

Annie gave her a warm smile. "You're very welcome."

"Go ahead, ask her," Gwendolyn urged her sister.

"Ask me what?" said Little Red Riding Hood.

Annie sighed. "My sister wants a hood like yours. We'd be willing to pay for it."

The girl's eyes lit up. "Granny could use the money. I'm sure she has a spare hood somewhere. Wait here and I'll go look."

"I don't know if I want someone's used hood," said Gwendolyn as they watched Little Red Riding Hood run back into the cottage. "I thought we were going to ask the girl's grandmother to make me one."

"We would have if she'd been here and able to whip

one up, but we're not waiting around for her to come back," Annie replied.

"I'm going to go talk to Beldegard," said Liam. "Don't take too long. I think I heard thunder in the distance."

Little Red Riding Hood came tearing out of the cottage, waving a dark green cape. "I found it!" she called and handed the cape to Gwendolyn.

The princess gave her a weak smile, then glanced at her sister. Annie dug a coin out of her knapsack and handed it to Little Red Riding Hood, who clutched it in her fist as if it were the most precious thing she'd ever seen. "Thanks!" she cried, and skipped back to the cottage.

Annie took the cape from Gwendolyn's hands and shook it loose of its folds. It was a well-worn garment with a few threadbare spots, but still, it was well-made and clean.

Gwendolyn rubbed the corner of the cape with her fingers and began to pout. "I don't like it. It's old and it's not pink."

"I know!" Annie said. "I think it's perfect!"

CHAPTER 8

BELDEGARD AND LIAM SEARCHED THE FOREST for the rest of the afternoon while Annie tried to help and Gwendolyn complained that her feet hurt. The Dark Forest was only a hundred acres, so by the time it began to get dark they had already tromped across most of it without seeing a sign of any dwarves.

"This is interesting," said Beldegard, snuffling the ground. They had just reached the northwest corner of the forest where the trees were taller and older than the rest.

"Did you find a dwarf footprint, my love?" asked Gwendolyn.

Beldegard shook his head. "No, just bear prints—some big, some little. It looks like a mother bear and her cub live around here."

The thunder that had been rumbling to either side of them for most of the afternoon sounded closer now and the sky was quickly growing darker. "We need to find shelter," said Liam.

"Huh," grunted Beldegard. "Just stay away from caves. Even I don't want to face a mother bear with a cub. They get riled easily."

"The trees are thinner in this direction," said Liam. "It looks like someone cut some down. Maybe we'll find a woodcutter's cottage where we can pay to spend the night."

"I'd rather sleep outside," murmured Gwendolyn.

"Not in the rain," Annie told her. "When this storm hits, you won't care what the cottage is like as long as you have a roof over your head."

"I don't think that's true," Gwendolyn said, but Annie noticed that her sister was quick to pull the hood of her new cape over her head when the first raindrops began to fall.

They continued to walk as the rain fell harder and were drenched when Liam finally shouted, "Over there! I see a house."

"I hope it's clean," Gwendolyn muttered under her breath.

"I hope they'll let us in," said Annie.

The house had two stories, arched windows, and an arched door. The fireplaces at either end of the house looked as if they were holding the sharply peaked roof in place. Outbuildings in the back included stalls for horses, but the only occupants seemed to be the barn swallows that Beldegard disturbed when he peeked inside.

"There are no lit candles or fires in the fireplaces," Liam told Annie as he peered through the windows. "Either no one is home or they've gone to bed already. Wait here while I look and see."

It was getting colder now, and though the cape kept Gwendolyn warm, Annie had begun to shiver. She drew closer to Liam as he pounded on the door. When no one answered, he shoved it open and stepped inside. "No one's here as far as I can tell," he said when he returned to the door a minute later, a lit candle in his hand. "Come in out of the rain, but stay by the door while I go look upstairs."

Liam took the candle with him, leaving the room dark once again. When Annie hesitated at the door waiting for her eyes to adjust, Gwendolyn pushed past her. Unfastening the ties on the soggy cape, Gwendolyn dropped it on the floor and walked off.

"Here," Annie said, handing the cape to her sister. "I'm not your servant. Hang it up somewhere so it can dry."

"Where?" Gwendolyn asked as she looked around.

Annie turned in place, examining the room. Only a little light came through the windows, so she really couldn't see much aside from a table with three chairs at one end and a grouping of three rocking chairs at the other. When she spotted candles and a flint on the mantel, she lit two and handed one to Gwendolyn. "Why don't you put your cape on the back of one of those chairs?" Annie said, pointing at the table.

Gwendolyn sighed as if Annie had asked for too much, but she walked to where she had pointed and draped the cape across the back of a chair. A small puddle began to form on the floor below the dripping cape. Annie started to look around for something to wipe it up, and noticed three bowls on the table, filled with some sort of food.

"There's no one upstairs either," Liam said as he came down the steps. "But I found three beds, so if you ladies would like to get some sleep, Beldegard and I can take turns keeping watch."

Normally Annie would have argued that she should share the burden of standing guard, but she was so tired that she didn't have the energy to protest. She turned to invite Gwendolyn to go upstairs with her, and found her sister examining the contents of one of the bowls.

"I think it's porridge," said Gwendolyn. "It's cold, but it's not bad. I mean, it's not moldy or anything." Picking up a spoon from the table, she poked the porridge with it. "Ugh, it's got dog hair in it."

"The whole place smells like wet dog," said Annie.

Gwendolyn stifled a yawn. "I don't see any dogs, though."

The door opened with a creak. Annie turned,

startled. Beldegard strolled in, took a long look around, and shook, splattering droplets on everyone. "There's no one here, but I found a saddlebag on the floor of the barn. It looks as if someone left in a hurry."

"Gwennie and I are going upstairs to sleep. Liam found some beds up there. Good night, you two," Annie said as she steered her yawning sister to the steps.

Even as she climbed, Annie could hear Liam and Beldegard talking. "It looks as if someone broke this rocking chair," said Liam. "Did you notice that everything is in sets of threes? I think a couple lives here with their child."

Although Beldegard lowered his voice, Annie could still hear him when he said, "I didn't want to say anything in front of the girls, but we should leave at first light. There's something about this place that you should know."

"It smells better up here," said Gwendolyn, and held her candle high. "At least the beds look nice. I'll take the big one at the far end."

"You go to bed," said Annie. "I want to go see what Liam and Beldegard were talking about."

"Don't you dare leave me alone up here!" said Gwendolyn. "I came up only because I thought you were going to bed, too!"

"All right," Annie said with a sigh. Whatever Beldegard was talking about, he didn't seem to think that it was so urgent that they couldn't stay in the house for the night.

Turning away from the stairs, Annie raised her candle. There were three beds in a row ranging from an extra-big one on the right to a smaller-than-normal bed on the left. Large trunks rested on the floor at the foot of each bed. Gwendolyn had already opened the lid of the trunk by the biggest bed and had started to root around inside.

"What are you doing?" Annie asked. "Those things belong to the owner of the house. You shouldn't go through them!"

"I'm cold, I'm wet, and I'm not going to spend another minute in these clothes," Gwendolyn said, plucking at her own sleeve. "You don't have to change if you don't want to. These are all men's clothes," she added, dropping the lid.

"It isn't right!" said Annie.

"I don't intend to take the clothes when we leave," Gwendolyn said, opening the trunk by the middle-size bed. "We'll just use them while we're here. If it would make you feel better, we can leave a coin to pay for their use. Oh, good. These will do just fine." She held up a sleeping robe of palest blue and tossed a white one to Annie. It was too big for her, but it was dry and as soft as kittens' fur when Annie rubbed it against her cheek. As princesses, of course, they had much finer clothes at home, but hadn't brought anything like this with them.

The rest of Annie's protests dried up unspoken. Following her sister's lead, she shed her wet clothes and slipped into the sleeping robe. "It's just for one night," she murmured as it warmed her chilled skin.

While Gwendolyn climbed onto the biggest bed, Annie set her candle on a small table and hopped onto the average-size bed, which poofed up around her like a lavender-scented cloud.

"I can't sleep on this bed!" exclaimed Gwendolyn. "The mattress is as hard as a rock."

"This mattress is much too soft," Annie told her.

Gwendolyn slipped off the biggest bed and ran to the smallest. "If this bed is any good, I claim it!" she cried out. She sat on the edge of the mattress for just a moment before lying down. Closing her eyes, she curled up on her side, murmured, "This bed is just right," and was fast asleep.

Her sister's breathing was already loud and steady when Annie blew out the candle and lay back on the too-soft mattress. Something crunched when she rested her head on the pillow. Reaching under it, she pulled out a sprig of rosemary. "At least it doesn't smell like wet dog," she murmured, and then she too was asleep.

❧

The sound of heavy footsteps on the stairs woke Annie. She lay quietly for a moment and let her gaze wander. The rain had stopped and the clouds had moved on, letting moonlight through the windowpanes. When she heard heavy breathing coming from both sides of her, she turned her head and saw that Liam was asleep on the big bed. Assuming that it was Beldegard coming to check on them, Annie turned over and closed her eyes again.

A board creaked by the foot of the smallest bed, claws scraped the wooden floor, and a child's voice piped up, "There's someone sleeping in my bed again!"

Annie sat up with a start as Liam rolled off the big bed, already drawing his sword. A dark figure was standing between the two largest beds. It wasn't big enough to be Beldegard. Neither was another, smaller figure even after it rose onto its hind legs. The figure snuffling Gwendolyn's feet was even smaller.

"Get behind me, ladies!" Liam shouted, brandishing his sword.

Annie glanced at her sister, who was lying on her back, staring at the menacing figures as if she were frozen in place. Scrambling off her bed, Annie grabbed her sister's hand and dragged her up and across the middle-size bed. She was shoving Gwendolyn off to the other side when someone latched on to Annie's ankle. When she tried to shake off whoever was holding her, the grip only grew tighter.

"I've got one!" cried the child's voice.

Suddenly Beldegard appeared at the top of the stairs. "What's going on up here?" he roared.

"They have a bear with them?" said the middle-size figure.

There was the scrape of a flint and a flame flared. Gwendolyn held up a lit candle. Annie would have thought she was dreaming if she hadn't felt the grip on her ankle. There were four bears in the room now. Beldegard was the largest by far, but two of the others appeared to be adults, while the one holding on to Annie was just a cub.

"Get away from my friends!" snarled Beldegard.

The middle-size bear growled and took a step toward Beldegard. "Are you threatening us in our own house?"

"Your house?" said Liam. "How could this be your house?"

"Mama, something's happening to me," said the bear cub.

"Not now, Teddy. Mama's busy," the middle-size bear replied. She was looking at Liam when she said, "We own this house and we don't take kindly to thieves!"

"We aren't thieves!" said Liam. "We came inside to get out of the rain. No one was here, so we thought the house was abandoned."

"It wasn't abandoned. Just this morning we went for a walk while our porridge cooled. We came home to find a girl had eaten Teddy's breakfast, broken his rocking chair, and was asleep in his bed. When we confronted her, she ran out of the house, taking my favorite gold necklace with her. We spent the whole day chasing her and when we finally gave up and came home, what do we find but more thieves sleeping in our beds!"

"Mama, look at me," cried the baby bear. "I have hands!"

"Not now, Teddy. I . . . You have what?"

"I'm scared," whimpered the cub. "Now my fur's going away."

"Eustace, go look at your son and see what he's talking about."

Annie squirmed around so that she was facing the cub. Even in the dim candlelight, she could see him changing. His ears were moving to the side of his head while his fur seemed to melt away. As each moment passed, he looked less like a bear cub and more like a seven-year-old boy.

"Liam, they aren't really bears," Annie said, scooting across the bed toward the little boy.

Knowing that they were really human made Annie less afraid of the bears. She stayed where she was when the father bear crouched beside his son and peered at his face.

"It's true!" said the father bear. "He looks like a human again!"

"Well, not quite," said Gwendolyn, "but he will if he keeps holding on to Annie."

The father bear's eyes flew to Annie's face. "Are you doing this? Are you a witch?"

Annie shook her head. "I can't do any magic, but magic doesn't affect me or anyone touching me."

"How can that be?" asked the mother bear as she padded toward her son.

"It was my only christening gift from a fairy," Annie explained.

"Annie is helping me on my quest," said Beldegard. "I'm human, too, but a dwarf turned me into a bear so he could steal my treasure. We're on a quest to find him."

The father bear's jaw dropped. "Did he have a long straggly beard and a raspy voice?"

When Beldegard nodded, the three bears began to talk at once.

"He was mean!" said the baby bear.

"He came to our house and demanded that we give him food and lodging. We might have done it if he hadn't been so rude!" the mother bear exclaimed.

"I told him to go away if he couldn't be polite," explained the father bear.

"He had another dwarf with him. That one was much nicer. He got mad and yelled at the bearded one. They left then, but the bearded one came back to steal our food. He frightened the servants so much that they ran off," said the mother bear. "He turned us into bears after that."

"How long ago was the dwarf here?" Liam asked.

"It's hard to keep track of time when you're a bear; the days sort of flow together," the father bear replied. "But I think it was less than a week."

Liam glanced from the mother bear to the father bear. "Is it possible that the dwarf is still in the Dark Forest?"

The father bear shook his head. "The Dark Forest isn't very big. I've been all over it since then, but the dwarf has definitely gone."

"Do you have any idea which way he might have headed?" asked Annie.

All three bears shook their heads.

"If I were you, I'd go see the fairy in the Moonflower Glade," said the father bear. "She can probably help you. Just be careful. The way to the Moonflower Glade is long and fraught with danger."

"I want to apologize for using your clothes without asking you first," Annie told the mother bear. "Ours were wet from the rain."

"That's perfectly all right, my dear," the mother bear told her. "It's not like I can use them now. If you find that dwarf and make him undo his magic, we'll be eternally grateful. Why don't you go back to sleep and I'll hang up your clothes to dry? Since we turned into bears, we've been sleeping downstairs. We just came up here to see what other damage that girl had done."

Annie helped the mother bear gather up the wet clothes, then watched her carry them down the stairs in her mouth. When all three bears had gone she climbed back into bed and was almost asleep when Liam and Beldegard began to talk in hushed voices.

"There's something I don't understand," said Liam. "If you were standing guard downstairs like you said you were going to, why didn't you see the three bears before they came upstairs?"

Beldegard cleared his throat, and when he spoke Annie thought he sounded embarrassed. "I went outside to take care of personal matters."

"What kind of personal matters would you need to tend to in the middle of the night when you're supposed to be standing guard?" Liam said, sounding cross.

"You know," said Beldegard, his voice so low Annie had to strain to hear it. "The kind a bear always does in the woods. I'm going downstairs now. I'll see you in the morning. And please don't tell the ladies about this!"

CHAPTER 9

THE MOTHER BEAR had already made porridge by the time Annie and Gwendolyn went downstairs the next morning. "It's the only food I can cook," she told them as they joined Liam at the table. "Eustace's fairy godmother gave us a magic cooking pot when we got married."

"She's only a minor fairy so all it will cook is porridge," said the father bear. "But it warms you up and fills your belly."

"Sounds tempting," Gwendolyn whispered to Annie, making a wry face.

Even so, with a little honey dribbled on top, the porridge was delicious and all the bowls were soon scraped clean.

"Before you leave, we were wondering if you could do us a favor," the father bear said to Annie as the travelers gathered outside the door. "Could we touch you all at once so we can see ourselves as we're supposed to be?"

"Yes, of course," Annie replied, and held out her hand. She was expecting them all to touch her hand or arm, but when the father bear nudged his cub toward her, the little bear stood on his hind legs and threw his arms around her waist. Annie staggered back into the mother bear's embrace, and then the father bear stood up behind the cub and Annie was enveloped in a big bear hug.

Annie glanced down and saw that the bear cub's fur was turning into silky brown hair. She heard the mother bear gasp behind her and felt the father bear's grip tighten as they too began to revert to their human form. And then the mother and father bears began to cry. She thought at first that they might be in pain, but when she looked at the father's face, she saw a middle-aged man smiling through his tears.

They'd been standing there for a few minutes when Annie began to wonder when they would let her go. Hot and uncomfortable, she fidgeted, hoping they would take a hint.

"I'm getting squished!" announced the little boy.

"Um," Annie began, "I think we should ..."

"I can't thank you enough!" cried the mother bear. "I thought I might never see their real faces again!"

Annie looked over her shoulder at the curly-haired woman with the tear-streaked face. "You're welcome,"

Annie told her. "Now if you don't mind, we really do have to go."

"Yes, of course," the mother bear said, and they all stepped back, freeing Annie.

The father picked up his son and put his other arm around his wife, pulling her to his side. "The Moonflower Glade is due north of here, but be careful."

"We will be," said Liam. "Can you be more specific about what dangers we might have to face?"

No longer in contact with Annie, the three people were already reverting back into bears. The half-man, half-bear father shook his head. "I've just heard that it's dangerous, not what the dangers might be. Good luck finding the evil dwarf. I don't know how you'll make him undo his magic, but he deserves whatever you do to him."

"Thank you again!" the mother bear called to Annie as the four friends started toward the path.

"That was really embarrassing," Gwendolyn told Annie when the bears were out of sight. "I thought they were never going to let you go, and the crying...I don't know how you stood it."

"They were happy!" said Annie. "There was nothing to be embarrassed about."

"Well, it made me uncomfortable, seeing them like that," Gwendolyn snapped.

They walked in silence for a few minutes, during which Annie kept expecting her sister to leave her side to walk with Beldegard. She was about to ask if she wanted something, when Gwendolyn turned back to her and cleared her throat. "I don't suppose that later, when we stop for a break or something, you could, uh—"

"Touch Beldegard's shoulder so you can gaze into each other's human eyes? Yes, I can do that," Annie said, and sighed.

ॐ

They had walked well into the afternoon when Annie finally turned to Liam and said, "Do you have any idea where we're going?"

"Not really," he said. "What about you, Beldegard? Do you think we're getting close?"

"I haven't a clue," said the bear prince.

"Then why don't we ask for directions instead of wandering around like fools?" Annie asked. "Surely we're far enough north that someone here knows where the Moonflower Glade is located."

Liam shrugged. "I suppose if you want to."

"Fine! I'm asking the first person we see!"

Annie would have been happy to talk to someone, but the path had become a road, and though it looked well traveled, they walked for miles without seeing a single person. She was becoming increasingly frustrated when she finally heard the creak of a wagon coming up behind them and spotted an old farmer driving a team of tired horses home from market.

While Beldegard hid in the bushes, Annie and her friends stepped aside so the wagon and horses could pass. "Pardon me, good sir!" Annie called. "Might I have a moment of your time?"

"Huh? Whazzat?" the old man asked, cupping his hand behind his ear.

"I was just wondering if you could give us directions. We're trying to find the Moonflower Glade," Annie said, raising her voice.

"You sure you want to go there?" asked the old man. "The way is long and fraught with danger."

"That's what we've heard, but we're not sure what it means," said Liam. "Will we have to pass some tortuous test or fight dragons or what?"

The old man shrugged. "I don't know what it means. It's just what everyone says. Never been there myself. Fact is, you can't get there from this direction. You'll have to go to the Old Mill Road, about a mile or two back," he said, pointing back the way they'd come. "Then turn left at the falling-down barn, which might have already fallen down, come to think of it, then go through Gruntly Village. Whatever you do, don't eat at the tavern with the bird on the sign. Eat at the other one, the food is good and someone there can give you directions for the rest of the way."

"Thank you, kind sir," said Annie.

"You're welcome, miss. By the way, did you know that a large animal is following you?"

Annie laughed and glanced toward the shrubs. "Yes, I know. He's a friend of ours."

The old man's eyes widened, but he just nodded and clucked to his horses to get them moving again, although Annie did hear him mutter to himself, "Now that's an odd one for you. Not as odd as those dwarves, though. Never heard such bickering in all my born days."

"Did you say you saw some dwarves?" Annie called after him, but he didn't seem to hear her and kept going.

"I guess you should have asked someone for directions sooner," Liam told her.

"But I...I mean, you...Oh, never mind!" she said, but she let him take her hand anyway.

Annie fumed all the way back to the Old Mill Road. Once they were seeing new scenery, however, she forgot to be irritated and began to look for the falling-down barn. The old farmer hadn't told them which side of the road to watch, but the others were looking as well and Beldegard was ranging across both sides of the road. It was the bear prince who finally came across the decaying timbers that had once been part of a barn. He emerged loping out of the underbrush, his tongue lolling like a big dog's, and plopped down in front of Annie. "I found the old man's barn. At least I think it was a barn. Come see for yourself."

Annie glanced at the waist-high grass and shook her

head. "I'll take your word for it. The farmer said we should turn left now. Do you see a road anywhere?"

"I saw something that might once have been a road. It's overgrown, but we could try it," said the bear prince. "What are we looking for next?"

"A village where we might get something to eat as well as more directions," Annie replied.

"So far the way to the Moonflower Glade hasn't been fraught with much of anything," said Liam. "I wonder what the bear and the old man were talking about."

"I'd rather we didn't find out," said Gwendolyn. "Walking this far is grueling enough without having to worry about dragons or monsters or some awful test."

"Have any of you ever heard of Gruntly Village?" asked Beldegard. "Because that might be it up ahead."

They peered through the trees in the direction the bear prince was facing. Although they couldn't see them very well, there were buildings just past the curve in the road.

"I don't know anything about it," said Liam. "So it can't be in Dorinocco. We must have crossed the border into Floradale."

"I remember now!" Annie exclaimed. "The fairy Moonbeam is the fairy in the Moonflower Glade! Mother was born in Floradale, you know, and Moonbeam was her favorite fairy godmother. Moonbeam was also the fairy who gave me the gift of no-magic."

"I don't recall Mother mentioning that," said Gwendolyn.

Annie sighed. "Then maybe she didn't tell you about it. She did talk to me once in a while when you weren't around."

"This is where I leave you again," said Beldegard. "I'll see you when you're finished in the village."

"Good-bye, my sweet," Gwendolyn said, hugging Beldegard around the neck. "Be safe."

"I live but to see you again," Beldegard told the princess, and licked her across her face.

"I feel ill," Liam muttered to Annie as they began to walk.

"I know! All that bear drool!" said Annie. "Imagine!"

"I meant I feel sick because of what he said. Being a bear must be affecting his mind. No self-respecting man would talk like that."

"Unless he's being *romantic*," Annie replied, giving Liam a wistful look.

"Is that what you call it?" said Liam. "Say, is it me or are those buildings larger than most?"

Annie sighed and shook her head. *Nice way to change the subject!* she thought, turning to look where he was pointing. From a distance the buildings hadn't looked like anything extraordinary, but as they drew closer she could see that they were proportioned differently than most. Some of the buildings had strange peaks and angles, while others had windows in odd places, as if the rooms inside weren't where you'd expect. All of the buildings, however, were taller than those she had seen in other villages.

"Look at how tall those doors are," said Gwendolyn, coming up from behind. "You don't suppose giants live here, do you?"

"Not giants," said Liam. "A giants' village would have doors twice as tall as these. If I'm not mistaken, this is an ogre village."

The color faded from Gwendolyn's face. "I didn't know ogres lived in villages. Maybe we should go around it."

Annie shook her head. "We need to ask for directions again. Look, there's a tavern with a bird on the sign."

"And there's another tavern over there," said Liam. "There's a bird on that sign, too. I thought the farmer said that only one sign had a bird on it."

"Someone must have changed the other sign," Annie said, frowning. "Now what do we do?"

"You two stay here and I'll go check out the taverns," Liam told the girls. "You should be fine if you don't talk to anyone."

Because there was only one street in the village and it seemed to be deserted, Annie didn't think they needed to worry. But just minutes after Liam disappeared into the closest tavern, a trio of young male ogres came out of one of the houses and sauntered over to where Annie and Gwendolyn were standing in the shade of a tree. All three of the ogres were nearly seven feet tall; Annie and Gwendolyn had to look up to see their faces.

"Well, well, well! What have we here?" said the ogre with one eyebrow across his forehead and the beginnings of a scraggly beard.

The second ogre grinned. Annie couldn't help but let her eyes wander to the top of his head, where stringy hair grew in patches around irregular bald spots. "Looks like two little humans wandering around all by themselves," growled the ogre.

"Do you know how dangerous that can be in a village like this?" asked the first ogre.

The third ogre laughed, an unpleasant sound that revealed his tongue, which was split down the middle like a snake's. When he saw that the girls were looking at him, he licked his lips and said something garbled that Annie couldn't understand.

The first ogre punched him in the arm, then turned to the girls and said, "Don't pay any attention to Screely. He cut his tongue because he thought it would make him look scarier. Now he can't talk worth dragon dung."

"We're not alone," Gwendolyn piped up. "We're here with friends."

"Really?" said the ogre with the bald spots. "I don't see anyone else. They must be invisible friends."

"Maybe they're imaginary friends," said the first ogre. "Do you have good imaginations?"

"Very good," said Gwendolyn. "I can imagine exactly what will happen to you if I scream and our friends come running."

The ogre with the bald spots snorted. "Oh, really?" he said, and stepped closer until he towered over both of the girls.

Annie didn't like the way the conversation was headed, and was relieved when she saw that an older ogre was hobbling toward them, using a whittled tree trunk as a cane. "What's going on here?" he snarled.

The three younger ogres backed away. "Nothing, Gloover. We were just greeting these two humans."

"You've talked to them long enough. Off with you before I take my cane to your backsides. So," he said to Annie and Gwendolyn once the other ogres had scuttled off. "What are you doing here? We don't get many humans coming this way."

"We just wanted directions," said Annie. "We're going to see the fairy Moonbeam, in the Moonflower Glade."

"Ah!" said the ogre. "I can give you directions, but you do know that the way is long and fraught with danger?"

Annie sighed. "Everyone keeps telling us that."

"All right then. Pay attention. Take the road out of town, go right at the pasture where Midas keeps his cattle, then go over the rainbow bridge, under the waterfall, turn left, and you're there."

"Are there any special dangers we should expect to find?" asked Annie.

"I don't know," said the ogre. "I've never been there."

"Annie, is everything all right?" Liam asked, hurrying across the street.

Annie nodded. "This nice gentleman was just giving us directions to the Moonflower Glade."

"Good, because no one in that tavern would talk to me. I've been waiting this whole time for someone to notice that I was there."

"I'm sure they noticed you," said the ogre. "They just didn't want to talk to you."

"Thank you for the directions," Annie told him.

"Good luck getting there," the ogre said, and walked away.

"Why does everyone keep warning us about the way to the Moonflower Glade?" Liam asked as they started down the road. "We have yet to see anything dangerous."

"I thought that ogre with the terrible tongue looked dangerous," said Gwendolyn.

Liam scowled at her. "I thought I told you not to talk to anyone."

"They talked to us first," Gwendolyn said, shrugging.

Chapter 10

Beldegard didn't rejoin them until they were out of sight of the ogre's village. Although he gave Gwendolyn an affectionate lick on her cheek, Annie thought he looked worried. Liam must have thought so too, because the first thing he said to the bear prince was, "What's wrong?"

Beldegard glanced back into the forest behind him. "I think someone is following us. I noticed it in the woods after you left."

"Maybe it's the boy with the cat Annie and Liam told me about," said Gwendolyn. "Maybe he discovered who I was and wants to start courting me."

"I doubt it was him," said Annie. "I don't think he ever saw you."

"What boy?" growled Beldegard.

"It might be one of the men from the ferry," said Liam. "Some of them seemed awfully interested in

Gwendolyn. But don't worry," he told the girls. "Now that we know someone is there, we'll watch for him. It would be hard to hide from all of us."

"Where do we go now?" asked the bear prince.

"We stay on this road until we reach a field where some man keeps his cattle," said Annie. "Then we turn right and cross over a rainbow bridge and go under a waterfall. It didn't sound as if it was too far from here."

"So when do we encounter all these dangers everyone keeps telling us about?" Gwendolyn asked.

"No one seems to know," Annie told her.

❦

The day grew hotter as they walked, so when the road eventually drew close to a stream, Gwendolyn cried out with delight and started for its banks.

"Wait!" shouted Beldegard as he lumbered after her. "You never know what might lie in wait in places like this. Remember, we've had all those warnings about danger." He padded around the clump of birch trees shading the water to snuffle the inviting moss edging the stream. When he bent down to taste the clear, sparkling water, he drew back suddenly and shook his head. "Don't drink this!"

"Why? Is it poisoned?" asked Liam.

"No," the bear prince said. "But cattle have fouled the water near here. This stream isn't fit to drink."

Annie's eyes lit up. "Oh, good!" she cried. "We must

be getting close to the spot where we're supposed to turn."

"But I'm thirsty!" wailed Gwendolyn.

"We all are," Annie told her. "It won't hurt us to go a little longer without water. We can probably drink when we're upstream of the cows, don't you think, Beldegard?"

The bear prince shrugged. "Maybe."

Gwendolyn was still grumbling when Annie led her back to the road. When they continued on and there was still no sign of the cattle, their feet began to drag. "Maybe Beldegard was wrong," said Gwendolyn. "We could still go back to the stream for a nice long drink."

"We're probably close," said Annie. "Look, there are people over there. We can ask them."

"I don't think—" Liam began, but Annie was already hurrying to the fence that divided the road from the land beyond.

"Excuse me!" Annie called, leaning up against the fence while she waved at the small crowd standing in the shade of an old oak tree. "I need some directions."

The sun was lowering in the sky, its rays shining into Annie's eyes, making it harder to see. She cupped her hand over her eyes and called to the people again, but they all kept their backs to her and remained huddled together. The few who seemed to be walking around aimlessly ignored her as well.

"They're very rude," Gwendolyn said at her side.

"Maybe they didn't hear me. I could climb the fence and go closer to talk to them," said Annie. "But did you notice how odd they're acting? They're just standing around, doing nothing. Look over there. Some are asleep in the grass."

"Honestly, I don't think they're going to be any help at all," Gwendolyn told her.

A loud snort made both girls turn their heads. One of the men who had been by himself was coming in their direction. Annie squinted, trying to see him better in the sun's glare. He was bigger than the rest, with bulging muscles and a head that … Annie gulped and stepped back from the fence, pulling her sister with her. This wasn't a person, it was a minotaur, with the body of a human and the head of a bull.

A roar broke the quiet of the afternoon as the minotaur came rushing at the fence, his head lowered. Annie and Gwendolyn fell back to the road while Liam ran to stand in front of them with his sword raised. Although their attacker slammed into the fence, bellowing, he made no further effort to reach them.

The group standing under the oak tree turned their heads. Annie shuddered. They were minotaurs as well, mostly adult females with a few children and two or three adolescents.

"These must be the cattle the ogre mentioned," said Annie, her mouth so dry that her voice sounded odd.

"There should be a road near here where we can turn right."

"As long as we don't have to go through that field," said Gwendolyn. "I'm glad you didn't hop the fence to go talk to them, Annie."

"So am I!" Annie told her, casting one more glance at the minotaurs.

Annie and Gwendolyn were careful to keep their distance from the fence and the now-watchful minotaurs, but Liam and Beldegard eyed the occupants of the pasture with interest. The beast with the head of a bull kept pace with them on his side of the fence, snorting and pawing at the ground if they stepped off the road. Eventually even he lost interest and left to rejoin his herd. Annie was relieved when he was gone, and began to enjoy the scenery, knowing that they were going the right way.

They were out in the open country now, with crops growing on one side and the fence on the other. Bees hovered around the wild roses covered with small white flowers that hugged the fence. Crickets chirped in the tall grass edging the fence, adding their song to that of the bees. Small birds flew dipping, curving patterns as they caught insects, while a hawk circled overhead, casting its shadow on the dusty road. The hot sun beat down, making Annie long for the shade they'd left behind. A trickle of perspiration ran down her spine, and she wiped her forehead with the back of her hand.

When they finally reached the corner of the pasture where the fence turned, they found a narrow dirt path leading off to the right. They walked single file now with Liam in the front and Beldegard bringing up the rear. Eventually they reached the end of the pasture where the fence turned away from the path, and soon after that the stream looped toward them. Once again Beldegard sniffed the water. After taking a tentative taste, he turned to the sisters and said, "You can drink now."

Gwendolyn ran to the water's edge and knelt down. Annie sighed and trudged after her. Liam followed, looking as hot as Annie felt. "I saw colored light reflecting off something up ahead," he said, laying his sword on the grass so he could bend down to drink. "It might be the bridge." He sipped from his cupped hands twice before adding, "When we reach the bridge, stay back while I look around. Trolls lurk under bridges, and they're nasty creatures at the best of times."

"Have you ever fought a troll?" asked Annie.

Liam nodded. "Yes, and I've been lucky to get away with my life each time."

"Don't worry," said Beldegard. "I'll be there and trolls don't scare me."

"Have you ever fought a troll?" Liam asked him.

"No, but I've seen plenty over the last two years. They run away when they see me coming."

"You are fierce looking, my darling prince," Gwendolyn said, stroking his furry back.

"Or they think a bear wouldn't have anything worth fighting for," Liam murmured in Annie's ear.

❧

Even before Annie spotted the bridge, she saw colors shimmering above the stream. Red, blue, purple, green, and yellow lights seemed to hang in the air, and when she got closer she saw why. The bridge that arced above the stream wasn't very long, but it was made of precious stone laid in stripes that sparkled and glimmered in the sunlight. Bands of ruby, sapphire, amethyst, emerald, and topaz ran from one side of the bridge to the other. Because the stones were transparent, it was easy to see that there weren't any trolls hiding under the bridge.

"This is beautiful!" Gwendolyn exclaimed. "But I don't understand why the ogres from the village haven't broken it up and carted it away."

"Magic," said Annie, who could hear the soft melody playing over and over again. "It probably keeps it intact and wards off blows that might break it. I suppose I'll have to sprint across it so I don't wreck the darn thing. Why can't fairies make regular bridges like ordinary people? Do you see how slippery this thing looks?"

"I don't have to run across, do I?" asked Gwendolyn.

Annie shook her head. "No, but you should go first in case I weaken it."

"I'll walk with you, Gwendolyn," declared Beldegard. "You can hold on to me."

The bear prince's first steps were tentative, and Gwendolyn moved even more slowly, but after a moment it became obvious that the magic that held the bridge together also gave it enough traction that it was easy to cross, and they hurried to the other side. Liam went next, although he kept glancing back at Annie as if to make sure no trolls were going to attack her. The moment he reached the other side, Annie started across. She was nearly halfway when she felt the stones shift under her feet and heard the melody become ragged. Another step and her foot slipped so that she staggered and almost fell.

"Hurry, Annie!" Liam cried, and started to come back for her.

"No, stay there!" she shouted as she took another step. The stones were like slick ice now, so slippery that it was impossible to keep her footing. Her feet skittered under her and it was all she could do to remain upright.

"Here, catch this!" Liam shouted, tossing the end of a rope he'd pulled from his knapsack.

Annie looked up as the rope sailed toward her. She caught it with one hand, but doing so made her lose her balance and she fell, landing on her knees and sliding toward the edge of the bridge.

"Hold on!" Liam called.

He began to drag her toward his side of the bridge, but Annie was too close to the edge. She scrabbled at the smooth surface, trying to get a grip, but slipped over the side and fell through the air into the stream. As the cold water closed over her head, she held on to the rope and used it to pull herself to the surface. Spluttering, she kicked out with her feet and stubbed her toes on the streambed. She stood and glanced down; the stream was only chest deep.

Annie waded to the side, shivering from the cold water, and let Liam take her hand and haul her onto the bank. He looked worried and didn't seem to notice that Annie got his clothes wet when he pulled her into his arms. Being so close to Liam felt good, warm, and right, and when Annie tilted her head back to gaze into his eyes, she thought for a moment that he was about to kiss her. Instead, he let go of her suddenly and stepped away, leaving Annie feeling colder than before.

Annie was confused. Liam had said such sweet things when they were in the Gasping Guppy, but they had been interrupted and he never had finished what he was about to say. Now he wouldn't even kiss her. In fact, she didn't think he had kissed her since they started their expedition. Was it something she had done? Maybe he had changed his mind about her.

Beldegard was already ranging ahead with Liam close behind when Annie began to walk. She scarcely noticed that the melody of the bridge was playing again.

"Are you all right?" Gwendolyn asked, eyeing her with concern.

"I'm fine," said Annie. She glanced down at her wet clothes, then gave her sister a rueful grin. "That was one way to cool off, although I wouldn't recommend it."

❧

It was late afternoon when the path took them alongside a stream, wider than the first and deeper. They soon heard the muffled roar of a waterfall, which grew louder as they walked. After that it wasn't far to the spot where water cascaded from atop a rocky cliff, sending a cloud of mist and spray high into the air. Annie's clothes were nearly dry, but the mist settled on her hair and face, making her wet all over again.

"Are we supposed to go around this, or what?" asked Gwendolyn.

"We're supposed to go behind it, but the path ends here."

"Then there's probably a way through," said Beldegard. "If there's one there, I'll find it."

"Be careful!" Gwendolyn called as the bear prince disappeared into the underbrush at the bottom of the cliff. "I worry about him so much," she said, turning to Annie. "He's always willing to go headfirst into danger. Don't you think he's the bravest prince you've ever met?"

"He's brave all right," said Annie. "But I think a prince who isn't a bear and still puts himself in danger is even braver." She was looking directly at Liam when she spoke and she smiled when he turned to wink at her.

Gwendolyn tossed her hair over her shoulder. "Each to her own opinion," she said, and stalked away.

"It's right here!" Beldegard called, his head appearing among the foliage.

Liam held the branches back for the two princesses, and they all followed Beldegard through the underbrush. They had to go only a few yards before they reached the entrance to the cave.

"What now?" asked Gwendolyn. "Do we go out the other side?"

"There's a passage out the back, but there isn't any light," Beldegard told them. "Hold on to me, everyone. I'll show you the way. Except for you, Annie. If you touch me, I'll be less bear and more human. Right now, I want to stay a bear."

"I'll walk with Annie," Liam said, taking her hand.

Annie wasn't sure what to think. First he wanted to touch her, then he didn't, now he did again. She was so confused!

After the first few steps, the passage curved and suddenly it was so dark that Annie couldn't see anything, including Liam, who was right beside her. Raising her free hand, she felt for the wall of the cave and found it, cold and slightly damp, closer than she'd expected. They walked forward, sliding their feet until they hit something, then felt for another place to step. It wasn't long before she saw a glimmer of light ahead.

"There it is," she told Liam. "We've almost reached the opening."

They could walk faster now and in less than a minute they were outside under the hot sun. Liam let go of her hand the moment they left the passage. Annie tried not to sigh as he moved away.

"The ogre said we should turn left after this," said Gwendolyn.

Where the land on the other side of the waterfall had been cleared for crops and pastures, the land on this side was heavily forested. "I guess we should just follow the path for now," Annie said as they began to walk. "I don't see a . . . Wait. Are those moonflowers?"

What she had first taken for trees on the left side of the path were actually some of the most unusual plants Annie had ever seen. Long stalks higher than a tall man's head supported spheres the size of big pumpkins. Pale blue and iridescent white, the spheres seemed to float above them as if they were tethered to the ground rather than growing from it. A faint breeze made the spheres bump into each other, filling the glade with a gentle tapping sound.

"I think this might be the Moonflower Glade," said

Annie, stepping off the path. "Now all we have to do is find Moonbeam."

"That should be easy enough," Liam said as he followed her. Cupping his hands around his mouth, he shouted, "Fairy Moonbeam!"

There was no response.

"I don't think anyone is here," announced Gwendolyn. "Maybe this isn't the right place."

"What's going on?" asked a voice. "You don't have to make such a ruckus!"

"I hear someone, but I don't see anyone," said Gwendolyn.

"There's no need to be rude!" the voice said, and a sprite no taller than Annie's knee stomped between the moonflowers to stand in front of Gwendolyn. Scowling with his head thrown back and his hands planted on his hips, he looked outraged.

"Aren't you adorable!" Gwendolyn cooed, and crouched down so her eyes were level with his.

The sprite's face turned red so quickly that Annie was afraid he was going to hurt himself. "How dare you!" he said. "I am not 'adorable'!"

Annie grabbed her sister and pulled her away from the sprite. "Please excuse my sister. She's never met anyone like you before. She didn't mean to be rude."

"Huh," grunted the sprite. "Why are you here anyway? Are you nosy posies come to snoop around, or do you have a real reason?"

Annie glanced up as a light rain began to fall even though the sun was out. She was mesmerized when the moonflower blossoms opened to form a translucent roof that caught every drop of the sun shower. Looking through the blossoms from below, Annie saw patterns forming on the petals as the drops splashed and ran to the center, where they seemed to disappear.

"How beautiful!" she breathed.

"We came to see the fairy Moonbeam," said Liam.

"Well, you can't," said the sprite. "She's not here. And before you ask, I don't know when she'll be back. She's gone to the capital to help some girl get ready for the prince's ball. After that, she could go just about anywhere to help one of her charges. Now, if that's all you want, you should go."

"Could you answer one other question first, please?" said Annie. "Why did everyone tell us that the way to the Moonflower Glade was long and fraught with danger? It was long enough, but it wasn't particularly dangerous."

The sprite shrugged. "It's what Moonbeam tells people to discourage visitors. She hates unexpected guests."

The sun shower stopped as suddenly as it had begun. Annie looked up as the blossoms closed back into their spheres.

"Which way do we go to reach the capital?" asked Beldegard.

The sprite looked surprised. "So it *is* an enchanted bear! I wondered why he was with you. You go that way," he shouted at the bear prince, pointing to where the path turned right.

"I'm a bear, I'm not deaf," grumbled Beldegard.

"I was trying to be helpful," the sprite replied, and stomped off.

"I still think he's the cutest thing," whispered Gwendolyn.

"I heard that!" the sprite shouted.

Annie took hold of Gwendolyn's arm and hurried her onto the path. "We'd better go before you get us in real trouble!"

CHAPTER 11

FOLLOWING THE PATH that the sprite had shown them, they reached a well-traveled road in less than an hour. "I know this road," said Beldegard. "It's the main route from the north to the south end of Floradale. I've traveled it many times."

"Do you mean to tell me that we could have reached the Moonflower Glade by going this way?" said Liam as they stepped aside to let a wagon pass. "It would have saved us so much time!"

"But no one told us about it," said Annie. "Moonbeam probably doesn't mention it to people because she doesn't want them to drop in."

"Why would they want to?" said Liam. "And why would she care? It sounded like she's almost never home."

"At least we have some idea how to find her," said Gwendolyn. "All we have to do is locate the girl she's helping."

"And how do you suggest we do that?" asked Liam.

"We'll go to the ball and Annie can bump into each of the girls. The one who looks beautiful through magic will be the one that Moonbeam helped. When Annie touches her, the girl's magic will fade and we'll know. And don't worry. Getting into the ball will be easy. The crown prince of Floradale is our cousin."

"I've heard he's spoiled rotten," said Beldegard.

"Prince Ainsley is our mother's oldest brother's only son," said Annie. "We couldn't visit them when we were younger because our parents were afraid that Gwendolyn might touch a spinning wheel. They discouraged visitors, too, just in case one tried to slip a spinning wheel into the castle. We've never actually met Ainsley, but we have seen miniature portraits of him. He's handsome, of course, and I hear that he prides himself on his dancing."

"Which was probably a christening gift from a fairy, just like his good looks," said Liam. "He sounds like a real winner."

"You shouldn't make judgments about people before you meet them," Gwendolyn told him. "He might be very nice."

"Or he might be like most princes who received all their best qualities as christening gifts from fairies and never have to work for anything. But you're right, I shouldn't judge him before I meet him."

Beldegard said something to Gwennie that Annie

couldn't hear, but it made her sister laugh and bend down to kiss the bear prince's furry nose and receive a lick on her cheek in return. Annie glanced at Liam. He used to be spontaneously affectionate toward her, kissing her now and then and touching her arm or cheek when they talked, but something had changed. He hadn't shown any real sign of affection toward Annie in days. Sure, he held back branches for her and he'd tried to help her cross the bridge, but he would have done that for anyone. Lately he didn't seem to want to touch her unless he had to, and even then he stopped as soon as he could. If only she knew what was going on!

❦

They were standing on the side of the road, talking about what they should do next, when a carriage filled with revelers passed by. "You should get a ride to the capital with someone," said Beldegard. "You'll get into town a lot faster. I'll meet you by the south gate tomorrow."

"I hate that you can't go with us," said Gwendolyn.

"I wouldn't be of much use to you. No one will want to give a bear a ride, and I wouldn't fit in at the ball anyway." Beldegard made a strange wheezing sound, which Annie thought was the bear version of laughing.

"I know, my love. Annie," she said, turning to her sister, "could you touch Beldegard's shoulder so we can have one last kiss before he leaves? I won't see him again until tomorrow and—"

"Oh, look!" Annie exclaimed. "Here comes a farmer with a wagon. I'm sure he has enough room for three! We should ask him, Gwennie. There's no saying when another ride might come along, and you know we'll need time to get ready for the ball."

"I suppose . . . ," Gwendolyn said, turning back to the bear prince.

"I must go," he told her when she caressed his cheek. Nudging her hood off with his nose, he gave her one big slurp, licking her from chin to ear, before turning and heading for the forest.

"I'll see you tomorrow!" Gwendolyn called to his retreating back.

It took only a minute of negotiations for Liam to gain them seats in the back of the wagon. The farmer gave Annie and Liam cursory glances, although he couldn't seem to take his eyes off Gwendolyn. Her hood was still down and her hair was plastered to the side of her face. He watched as she waved good-bye to someone in the woods. When she turned back and noticed that the farmer was watching her, she was quick to pull her hood up before climbing into the wagon. The farmer sighed, then clucked to the horses to get them moving.

Annie was surprised by how much traffic was on the road. They passed a traveling minstrel wearing a lute strapped to his back. Armed knights rode on horseback alongside a gilded carriage, moving too quickly for Annie to see inside. A boy and an old man stopped by the side of the road were arguing about who should ride their donkey. Twice their wagon passed merchants riding with cavalcades of horses and carts bearing their goods.

Both Annie and Gwendolyn watched with great interest each time they approached another traveler, but Liam acted as if he had seen it all before. Covering his eyes with his cap, he took a nap leaning against a bushel of beets that bounced with each jolt from the uneven road. It wasn't far to the castle, but Liam seemed refreshed when they entered the walled city and he pulled his cap off his eyes.

Annie had seen a few castles during her hunt for Gwendolyn's prince, but none as grand as this. It rose on a hill above Loralet, glinting golden in the setting sun. Pennants flew from so many spires that Annie lost count as she gawked with her head thrown back like a tourist.

The farmer stopped his horses to let Annie, Liam, and Gwendolyn out of the wagon in the center of the city just outside the main castle gate. Annie was concerned that they might not be able to get past the guards, but Liam spoke with the men, demanding entrance in such a regal and commanding way that they quickly stepped aside. Once inside the castle, they found a servant to fetch the steward.

While Annie and Liam sat down to wait for the steward to appear, Gwendolyn seemed unable to sit still. After examining everything in the small antechamber, she paced the length of the room. "I can't wait to go to the ball!" she said, her eyes bright with excitement. "I've never been to a ball before. There will be lots of dancing, won't there?" she asked, turning to Annie and Liam.

Liam laughed. "There'll be one dance after another where you'll dance with people you've never met before and hope you'll never meet again. I haven't been excited about going to a ball in years, or maybe never. It wouldn't be so bad if you didn't have to talk to people, but most of them will bore you till your brain is numb."

"I don't care," said Gwendolyn. "At least I'll have the chance to dance with someone other than my dancing master and my ladies-in-waiting. And all the women will wear beautiful gowns and the men will be so handsome! I can't wait!"

"All I want is a hot meal and a hot bath," said Liam. "What about you, Annie?"

"I just want to find the dwarf and go home," she replied, watching her sister pace.

"We want that, too," said Gwendolyn. "But while we're here, we might as well enjoy ourselves."

Annie sighed. "That's true, as long as we don't forget why we're here."

"And why is that exactly?" asked a voice from the doorway. Annie looked up to see a man wearing the chain and medallion of a castle steward. "I understand you told Erwin it was most urgent that I come see you. I'm a busy man. We're putting on a ball tonight, or haven't you heard?"

Annie took off the cap covering her hair so that he could see that she was a girl. "My sister and I have come to visit our uncle and aunt, King Daneel and Queen Theodora."

"Oh, really?" said the steward. "You're dressed like farm boys and I'm supposed to believe that you're royal princesses? And who is he?" he asked, gesturing toward Liam. "The crown prince of Montrose who's been missing for two years?"

"This is Prince Liam, the crown prince of Dorinocco," said Gwendolyn. "You may tell our aunt and uncle that Princesses Gwendolyn and Annabelle of Treecrest are here."

The steward snorted in disbelief. "You expect me to believe that one of you is Princess Gwendolyn, the most beautiful princess in . . . Oh, my!" he said as Gwendolyn pushed the hood back from her face and pulled the cap from her hair. She smiled a slow, dreamy smile as she shook the tangles loose and let her hair tumble down her back.

"Pardon me, Your Highnesses!" said the steward, bowing low as he backed from the room. "I didn't know! I mean, I've never seen...I'll tell the queen of your arrival."

Gwendolyn giggled as the sound of the man's clicking heels receded down the hallway. "I've always wanted to do that. Did you see his expression?"

Annie nodded. "Many times, and always on men who are looking at you. I guess having you with us is proof enough."

"It seemed to be enough for him," said Liam.

༄

In only a few short minutes the steward was back with effusive apologies and an invitation to join the queen in her chambers. As they followed him through the corridors, Gwendolyn let her hood stay down. She smiled when people stopped to stare as she passed by. "I know people sometimes stared at home, but I was so used to it I didn't pay much attention," she whispered to Annie. "But after spending days hiding in that hood, this is kind of fun. I don't know how you can stand being ignored all the time."

"I've never been treated any other way," Annie replied. "When you're around, most people don't even look at me."

"I'm sorry," said Gwendolyn. "I never realized. I guess I just never thought about it."

"There you are, my darlings!" cried the queen as they entered a sun-filled chamber. "Welcome to Flora-dale!" Four of her ladies-in-waiting stood and left the room at a nod from the queen. A fifth woman continued to play a harp in the corner.

"Your Highness," murmured Annie. Both girls curtsied while Liam swept a deep bow.

Annie thought the queen looked nice. She was beautiful, of course, with dark brown hair and perfect features, but she also had kind eyes and a smile that made you want to smile, too.

"Let me look at you," said the queen. "Ah, yes, I can see that your parents hired a talented artist to paint your portraits. Yours looks just like you, Annie. But Gwendolyn, I'm afraid yours doesn't do you justice. You really are extraordinarily beautiful. I wish I could have met you girls before this, but that whole thing with spinning wheels ... Even so, your mother has written to me so much about you that I feel I know you already. And this is Prince Liam? I've heard about you as well. And what about the bear? Your mother told me that your true love is an enchanted prince, Gwendolyn. Is he here as well?"

The queen looked around as if she might see the bear lurking in the corridor behind them, but Gwendolyn just laughed and shook her head. "He doesn't like cities."

"Of course not! Particularly on a day like today.

Everything is in a shambles as we prepare for the ball. Oh, dear, how could I have forgotten! You must get ready for the ball. Ainsley will be so delighted that you're here in time to attend! Maud," she called to the lady-in-waiting, who set aside her harp and hurried over. "See to it that the servants get hot baths, food, and the appropriate clothes for our young guests." As Maud nodded and hurried from the room, the queen turned back to them saying, "Let them know if there's anything else you need. Now go! The ball begins in two hours."

CHAPTER 12

ANNIE GLANCED AT HER REFLECTION in the mirrored wall. The only other time she had worn a ball gown, she had been entered in a contest to win the hand of Prince Andreas for her sister. The gown she had worn then had looked delicate and sweet. This gown was bolder, with a lower-cut bodice and more form-fitting lines. A pale yellow, it had slashes of brilliant blue in its sleeves, and on the bodice and hem. It wasn't her favorite shade of blue, but it did go nicely with the yellow. She turned to check her reflection from the side. The gown looked as if it had been made for her and would do very well.

Gwennie, on the other hand, looked exquisite in a gown that hugged her perfect figure from shoulders to waist, where it swirled down to the floor in a cascade of rose over an underskirt of silver. The fabric shimmered in the candlelight and would have been gorgeous on a stick, but on the most beautiful princess in all the kingdoms it was entrancing. The maid who had styled her hair had let it fall in soft, gleaming curls down her back. She had put neither powder nor rouge on Gwendolyn's face because the princess didn't need it. Her skin was flawless, her cheeks were flushed with a natural pink, and her eyes glittered with ever-increasing excitement.

With all the time that had been spent on her own preparations, Annie knew she looked the best she had in her entire life. Unfortunately, she also knew that entering the ballroom with Gwendolyn meant that no one would even notice her, let alone what she looked like. Because she was the older sister, Gwendolyn would go in first. Annie might as well be invisible when she walked down the stairs.

She was waiting for her sister to reach the landing at the top of the steps when Liam entered the corridor. He looked magnificent in the blue jacket with the silver piping of Dorinocco royalty, and his bearing was that of a king's. Suddenly Annie understood why the ladies-in-waiting had chosen her ball gown. The blue was the same shade as Liam's jacket.

Annie was certain that even Liam wouldn't be able to resist Gwennie's allure tonight, but he never glanced her way. Instead, he kept his eyes on Annie, and the look he gave her made her heart beat faster. As he took her hand to lead her to the stairs, Annie gazed into his eyes and realized how much he had come to mean to her. She had never felt so strongly about anyone before and she wondered if this might actually be love.

When Gwendolyn reached the top of the stairs, Annie heard a collective gasp as everyone in the ballroom saw her sister at once. Liam squeezed Annie's hand and she smiled up at him. She no longer cared if every courtier in the castle ignored her. Liam was hers and he was all she wanted. Walking to the stairs hand in hand, she felt a warm glow inside of her that calmed her nerves and made her confident enough to go on.

Liam paused on the landing and gave Annie's hand another reassuring squeeze. "You are so beautiful," he whispered, sparking a ripple of happiness that started at her heart and washed through her. He looked as if he wanted to say more, but just then the herald announced their arrival in a loud and carrying voice.

When Liam turned to face the crowd below, Annie followed his example. A sea of strangers dressed in their brightly colored finest filled a room at least twice the size of the great hall at home. Turning back to Liam, she saw that his grin was genuine and it gave her the courage to descend the stairs, one slow step at a time. They were only partway down when she noticed that the crowd was moving as if currents carried them from one side of the room to the other, redistributing them by gender. Many of the men seemed to be drawn like cats to a dish of cream located near the foot of the stairs, while the women moved to get out of their way. Annie glanced down and saw what was drawing the men. Just as she suspected, Gwendolyn was the cream.

Annie and Liam had scarcely reached the bottom of the staircase when a young man took Gwendolyn by the arm and escorted her to the center of the room. From the glimpse Annie had caught of him, the young man appeared to be her cousin, Prince Ainsley. The floor around them cleared as the musicians at the far end of the room struck the first notes and Ainsley took Gwendolyn in his arms.

They were dancing one of the more modern dances like the one Annie had danced with Prince Andreas. Although it was a new dance, both Ainsley and Gwendolyn seemed to know it well, and they swirled across the center of the floor so gracefully that it was hard to look away. Annie did, however, noting that while the men were watching Gwendolyn with great longing, the women's eyes looked angry or disappointed.

The first dance had ended when Liam pulled Annie into the center of the floor. As the music began again, other couples joined them and soon they were caught up in a swooping, spinning romp across the room. They passed Gwendolyn and Ainsley twice. The prince's eyes were fixed on Gwendolyn's face with such adoration that it made Annie uncomfortable, but her sister seemed more interested in watching the other dancers around them.

When the dance ended, Annie leaned close to Liam and said, "It's time I start what I came here to do. I'm going to see if I can find that girl."

"Fine," said Liam, "but I'm going to claim you for another dance in a little while."

"I certainly hope so!" said Annie, and slipped off into the crowd lining the sides of the room. She walked among them smiling and talking to the women and girls while making polite excuses when men asked her to dance. Although she couldn't deny that she loved dancing with Liam, she was there to find the girl who could lead them to Moonbeam . . . and from there to that evil dwarf!

Everyone seemed friendly at first, welcoming her to Floradale and asking about Treecrest. Most of the girls seemed to be around her age, although some might have been a few years older. Annie decided that the women who were with them were mostly their mothers or aunts, and were there to encourage a match between the prince and their charges.

Everywhere she went, Annie bumped into people or brushed up against them in unobtrusive ways, watching to see if anything about them was altered by the disappearance of magic. A few girls changed slightly; one's nose grew longer and another's beautiful hair became lank and dull. Neither change was drastic enough to have warranted a fairy's last-minute intervention, however.

As she walked among them, Annie couldn't help but overhear snippets of conversations between people who didn't realize that she was there. She learned that she was right about the older women. She also learned how much they resented Gwendolyn.

"If that princess hadn't shown up, the prince would have been dancing with you right now!" one mother told her daughter.

"No one stands a chance with that princess here!" exclaimed another.

"Two princesses coming to the ball when we weren't expecting any! Why did we even bother to come?"

"You're both much prettier than the younger princess, but no one can compete with the older," said a woman with her back to Annie. When her daughters shushed her and pointed, she turned and saw Annie. Acting as if she'd done nothing wrong, the woman curtsied so low that her black wig shifted on her head. "Hello, Your Highness," she said. "Welcome to Floradale."

"Thank you," Annie said.

"My name is Lady Lenore Fauxliette, and these are my daughters, Lady Wilhemina and Lady Zelda."

"She called us 'ladies'!" the larger girl whispered to her sister in an overloud voice while jabbing her with her elbow. When her mother turned and glowered at her, the girl lost her smile and looked away. The other girl, as tall and thin as her mother, gave Annie a simpering smile.

"We're delighted that you were able to grace us with your presence this evening," Lady Lenore continued. "Unfortunately, it's awfully hot in here and will be getting hotter as the night goes on. Perhaps you and your sister won't be staying the entire evening?"

"I'm not sure how long we'll be staying," said Annie, trying to think of a way to leave the woman without being rude.

Lady Lenore was unable to hide her irritation when she said, "I see. Your sister seems to be enjoying her dance with our dear Prince Ainsley. She is aware that he is her cousin, isn't she?"

"I know people who married their cousins," said the larger girl, who was heavier, but had a nicer demeanor than her pinch-faced sister.

"Willie!" snapped her mother. "Don't speak unless you're spoken to! I'm sure the princess doesn't want to talk about such things."

Annie had had enough. She wanted to make her excuses and leave, yet she hadn't forgotten why she was there. It seemed highly unlikely that a fairy had used magic to help either of these girls get ready for the ball, but she might as well make sure.

"It was lovely to meet you," she said, and leaned forward to kiss Wilhemina on the cheek. When she stepped back, the girl looked surprised, as if she hadn't expected Annie to talk to her, let alone kiss her. But then Wilhemina lurched forward to plant a forceful kiss on Annie's cheek, surprising the princess with her vehemence. When the girl didn't change in any way, Annie turned to Zelda and kissed her cheek as well. Nothing happened. It wasn't until Lady Lenore looked as if she wanted a kiss that Annie said good-bye and walked away.

Annie was determined not to get caught up in another such conversation if she could help it, but suddenly two men were standing in front of her. "I am Lord Weatherby," said a large man with loud, booming voice. "May I have the honor of—"

"I was just about to ask her, Weatherby," said a smaller man with intense, dark eyes and thick, bushy eyebrows.

The two men were glowering at each other when a third stepped up, brushed them aside, and led Annie onto the dance floor without even asking. "I apologize, Your Highness, but I didn't think you wanted to witness their argument. Those two argue over everything, and are too tedious for words. My name is Lord Camril and I am the best dancer at the ball, other than Prince Ainsley, of course."

"I'm delighted to meet you, Lord Camril," Annie said, wishing she could have escaped him as well as the other two men.

"So what do you think of our fair kingdom?" he

asked as the music started and he led her into the first steps of the dance.

"The parts I've seen of it are lovely," said Annie.

"And what parts have you seen?"

"We came through the Dark Forest in the south."

Lord Camril looked confused. "Don't you mean the Black Woods? They are lovely, but they're located in Montrose to the west of here. I went there once to hunt wild boar with my uncle, who was a friend of the king. We never did see any boar, but we did meet a family of dwarves who owned a mine. The entire family worked in it. Wait, I do seem to recall another forest with a similar name to the south. It's much smaller than the Black Woods, and not nearly as interesting. Look! There's Weatherby dancing with the younger Simplin girl. He does look angry, doesn't he?"

Before Annie could ask Lord Camril about the dwarves, the dance carried her away, handing her from one partner to another until she finally ended up with the nobleman again just before the dance was over. Seeing Liam waiting for Annie, Lord Camril bowed to her and was about to leave when Annie stopped him, saying, "Those dwarves—what else can you tell me about them?"

The nobleman shrugged and said, "Nothing really. It was a large family, all boys. It happened years ago. I remembered it because my barber said he was south of the city on his way home from visiting relatives last week when he saw a pair of dwarves."

"Really?" said Annie. "And where were they going?"

"I really couldn't say," said Lord Camril. After giving her an odd look, he bowed again and disappeared into the crowd.

Three young men were approaching when Liam took her by the hand. "What was that about?" he asked as he led her off to another part of the dance floor.

"That man told me about some dwarves he'd met. He said that two dwarves were seen south of the city just last week."

"It doesn't mean they were the same two dwarves," Liam told her. "There have to be others around as well. Blast, that woman is headed this way dragging her daughter behind her. Listen, Annie, I need you to rescue me. When you left, all the matchmaking mamas descended on me, hoping I'd fall in love with one of their daughters. I've danced with far too many of them already tonight, when the only person I want to dance with is you."

"I would love to dance with you," said Annie.

They were wending their way through the crowd when Annie heard one mother talking to another. "I'm thinking of taking Louisa home soon. There's no point in staying when Prince Ainsley isn't going to dance with anyone but that princess and we're paying for that rented coachman and carriage by the hour."

"I know what you mean. I was just telling Portia the same thing," said the woman beside her.

"I can't dance with you now," Annie whispered to Liam. "I have to go talk to Gwennie."

"Then I'll go with you," he said, and began to peer through the crowd at the couples on the dance floor. They found Ainsley and Gwendolyn by following everyone's eyes to the beautiful couple moving as if they were floating in a room filled with plodders. When the dance ended, Annie and Liam made their way to where Gwendolyn was laughing at something the prince had said.

"Gwennie, I have to talk to you," said Annie.

"But I was talking to Ainsley!" Gwendolyn said, still smiling up at the prince. It wasn't until he turned a questioning gaze on Annie that Gwendolyn told him, "This is my sister, Princess Annabelle."

"Ah, another cousin!" said the prince. "I'm delighted to meet you at long last."

Annie was surprised when he took her hand in his and kissed the back of her fingers, showing her two things that she hadn't known. First, that Ainsley hadn't heard the rumors about how touching her diminished one's magic, and secondly, that the prince would have been a pudgy young man with crooked teeth if magic hadn't made him handsome.

"I'm happy we finally met as well," said Annie. Pulling

Liam forward, she stepped aside, saying, "And this is Prince Liam of Dorinocco. Why don't you two get acquainted while I talk to Gwennie?"

"You have to leave," Annie said in her sister's ear even as she pulled her aside. "Say you have a headache or something, and go up to your room."

"But I don't want to!" Gwendolyn said, looking shocked. "I feel fine and I'm having such fun! Oh, Annie, everyone has been so nice to me and Prince Ainsley has danced every dance with me, but I can tell that others want to because they keep coming up and..."

"You have to, Gwennie," Annie told her. "Ainsley is spending all his time with you when he's supposed to be dancing with these girls. If he doesn't start dancing with them, they're going to leave, then we'll never know who the girl was and we won't be able to find Moonbeam. Remember why we're here. Remember Beldegard!"

At the sound of Beldegard's name, Gwendolyn's face flushed pink and she shook her head. "You're right, Annie. I'm not here to enjoy myself. I'll go to my room while you find the girl. But please try to find her soon so I can come back to the dance?"

"I'll try," Annie said with a laugh.

While Gwendolyn made her excuses to Prince Ainsley, Annie and Liam returned to the dance floor. She noticed that the prince looked disappointed when her

143

sister left, but it wasn't long before he was dancing with another young lady.

Suddenly the mood in the ballroom changed. The prince was available again; the young ladies had a chance after all. Expressions brightened, voices grew joyful, and no one left early. The dance floor became more crowded now as young men sought other partners, having given up on the idea of dancing with Gwendolyn.

After their dance, Annie and Liam separated again, Annie to mingle with the women, while Liam danced with yet another girl whose mother watched eagerly from the side. Once again Annie bumped into girls or brushed against their arms or touched them in the most inconspicuous way she could manage, but aside from the changes in their appearance that Annie had expected, nothing really happened.

Annie was sure the change had to be unusual. Daughters of the nobility and the wealthy were given magical gifts of physical beauty soon after they were born. None of them would have required help so close to the prince's ball. Whoever Moonbeam had helped would have needed assistance of another sort.

By the time Liam asked her to dance again, Annie was frustrated and ready to give up. After touching nearly every girl in the ballroom with no luck, she was afraid that she would never find the one she wanted. "I don't know what to do," she told Liam as they tried to find a clear space on the dance floor. "I've tested nearly every girl here."

Liam shrugged. "I'd help you if I could but...Watch out! Ainsley isn't looking where he's going. His partner is about to..." Liam tried to maneuver Annie out of the way, but with nowhere to go she couldn't avoid the prince's partner as he twirled her around.

"Ow!" Annie cried as the girl bumped into her and stepped on her foot with a glass slipper.

"I'm so sorry!" the girl said, retracing her steps to check on Annie. "Are you all right?"

When Annie staggered as she tried to look at her foot, the girl put her hand on her arm to steady her. "Annie, look," said Liam, and she raised her eyes.

The beautiful white gown the girl was wearing had begun to change. What had been silky white fabric embroidered with tiny silver stars became the stained and ragged gown of a servant girl from a less prosperous house. In place of glass slippers she wore scuffed brown shoes riddled with holes. The jeweled necklace at her throat turned into a dandelion chain. All the silver stars holding her hair on top of her head turned into pieces of mica that dropped to the floor, allowing her hair to fall loose around her shoulders. Somehow, even though her clothes were tattered and worn, she remained one of the prettiest girls there.

"Oh, no!" the girl exclaimed when she glanced down. "Moonbeam told me this wouldn't happen until midnight! I can't ... I don't ... I have to go!"

With a cry of anguish, the lovely young girl fled to the stairs, where she stumbled on the first step, losing one of her shoes. Everyone was watching as she ran up the stairs. When she'd disappeared through the door, the buzz of gossip began.

Annie and Liam followed Prince Ainsley to the stairs and watched as he picked up the shoe. He nearly dropped it when it turned back into the delicate glass slipper.

"Who was that girl?" asked Annie.

"I have no idea," said Ainsley, "but I'm going to find out! I'll visit every cottage in the kingdom if I have to. Every girl in the land will try on this shoe until I find the right one! Even if I must—"

"We'll accompany you when you go," said Liam. "We want to find her, too."

"Now I feel bad," said Annie as her cousin walked away, looking forlorn. "They were having such a good time!"

"It wasn't your fault. She was the one who bumped into you!" Liam replied.

"But if we hadn't been here, they would still be dancing." She sighed when she saw the way Ainsley was gazing at the glass slipper in his hand. "I think he really liked her."

"And he wouldn't have known it if you hadn't made Gwennie leave."

Annie's gaze flickered toward the stairs. "I suppose Gwennie can return to the dance now. We did find the girl."

"Gwennie will be happy," said Liam.

"At least someone will," Annie told him, glancing back at her cousin.

CHAPTER 13

THE NEXT MORNING, Liam, Annie, and Gwendolyn were sitting in one of the lesser halls, eating a simple breakfast of fruit, dried fish, and dark bread when the fairy Moonbeam appeared beside them with a tinkling of silver bells.

"How dare you interfere with one of my ongoing projects!" she shouted at Annie and Gwendolyn, her plump cheeks quivering with rage. "Eleanor and the prince were supposed to spend the whole evening dancing in each other's arms and fall in love last night. Then you had to show up so he didn't want to dance with anyone but you!" she said, glowering at Gwendolyn. "And you," she said, turning back to Annie, "I don't know how you managed it, but you undid everything I'd done to get her ready. Her beautiful clothes weren't supposed to revert back to their original forms until midnight, after she'd won the prince's heart and left the castle. Now she's lost that air of mystery so essential to catching a prince, and everyone knows who she is."

"We're sorry," said Annie. "We just wanted to ask her how to find you, but then her clothes changed and she ran off. Believe me, not everyone knows who she is. The prince certainly doesn't, so your mystery is still intact."

"And from what we saw after the girl left, the prince was already smitten," said Liam.

"Really? Then perhaps we can redeem this mess. Wait, did you say you did all this just to find me? Why?" the fairy asked, narrowing her eyes at Annie.

"We're trying to help my true love find the dwarf that turned him into a bear," said Gwendolyn. "We were told you might be able to help us."

"Who told you that?"

"It was a bear named ... What was his name? Do you remember?" Gwendolyn asked, glancing from Annie to Liam.

"It doesn't matter," snapped Moonbeam. "I'm not answering any questions for you until you clean up the mess you made. The prince has to go find Eleanor so they can fall in love."

"How are we supposed to make them fall in love?" Annie asked.

"Don't worry about that part," said the fairy. "You get him there and I'll do the rest."

Annie shrugged. "We were going to search for Eleanor today anyway. I don't suppose you could tell us where to find her?"

"No! The prince has to make some effort or the spell won't work nearly as well. Just be sure that he finds her and that you don't mess it up any more than you already have!"

⁊

Annie, Liam, and Gwendolyn were wearing their old traveling clothes when they joined the prince in his search for Eleanor. One servant went with him to carry the glass slipper on a velvet cushion, along with three guards to fend off beggars, ruffians, and the mothers of the girls he hadn't claimed as dancing partners. Annie kept her sister in the back of the group, hoping she wouldn't distract the prince again.

They started at a large house at one end of town where a guard asked the servant who answered the door if there was an Eleanor in the household who had attended the ball the night before. The servant fetched a middle-aged woman. The prince was quick to make his excuses and leave.

"Next time ask if there are any *young* ladies named Eleanor who attended the ball," Prince Ainsley told his servant.

"Of course, Your Highness," the servant said, his mouth twitching as he tried not to laugh.

After that they went from house to house, asking for young ladies. They were visiting houses on the second street when a serving maid with freckles and laughing eyes answered the door and told them that no one else was at home. "But maybe I can help you. Who are you looking for?" she asked.

Prince Ainsley waved forward the servant carrying the glass slipper. "We're looking for the girl who wore this last night. Do you know anyone whose foot would fit in this shoe?"

"Isn't that pretty! It doesn't look very practical, though. It might break if you stomped your foot down hard, or be slippery if the floor was wet. It doesn't look like it would bend when you walked, so it would be uncomfortable, too. I do know a couple of girls it might fit. Could you be more specific? What does this girl look like?"

"She has golden curls and deep brown eyes and is named Eleanor," said Annie.

"I know a girl who looks like that, but they call her Cinderella. She works as a serving girl in a house near here, although her rightful place is at the table, not waiting on it. Her father was the master of the house. He died soon after he brought home a new wife who treats her daughters like royalty and makes Cinderella do all the work. The house is there," she said, pointing down the street. "The stone one—third house from the corner."

༅

The prince looked excited as they returned to the street. He walked faster now and everyone else had to run to keep up. They were striding down the left side of the road, looking for the house built of stone, when a young woman came storming out of the butcher's shop.

"Don't ask me again!" she cried. "I told you, Mother will pay you the next time she visits your shop."

The man who followed her out of the shop was shorter than the girl, almost as short as Annie. A blood-stained apron stretched across his rotund stomach and hung nearly to the ground. "But your mother never comes to my shop," the butcher said, his three chins quivering. "She always sends that girl Cinderella! Why isn't the girl here today? She's much nicer than you and doesn't demand better cuts of meat even when I give her the very choicest."

"She did something bad and is being punished," said the young woman.

Annie took a step closer. The young woman looked so familiar. It was Zelda, the daughter of that awful woman she had met the night before. If Eleanor—or Cinderella—had anything to do with them, Annie felt doubly sorry for her.

"Huh," said the butcher, scratching the bald spot on his head. "Well, you tell your mother that I want to be paid. I'm supporting three grown children of my own and I need the money. How do people expect me to stay in business if they don't pay me?"

Zelda glanced at the people passing by. When her eyes turned to the prince, she hurriedly curtsied while the butcher bowed low.

"There it is," said Ainsley, who hadn't noticed Zelda or the butcher. "The stone house three from the corner."

One of the guards hurried ahead and was already pounding on the door when the prince arrived. It was the Lady Lenore who answered, smoothing her dark, silver-streaked hair and looking annoyed. Her eyes widened in surprise when she saw the prince. "Your Highness!" she said. "What an honor!"

"Bring out the girl named Eleanor," said the guard. "She needs to try on a shoe."

The servant carrying the velvet pillow stepped forward and held up the shoe for Lenore to see.

"I'm sorry, but there's no one here by that name, although I see one of my lovely daughters behind you, and my other daughter is here somewhere." Turning her head, Lenore shouted "Willie!" over her shoulder.

"I'm going to look around back," Liam whispered to Annie, and he slipped down the narrow alley between the stone house and its neighbor.

"What do you want now, Mother?" came her daughter's reply.

"Come join us, sweet girl!" Lenore trilled. "Prince Ainsley is here to see you!"

"No, I'm not," said the prince. "I'm here to see Eleanor. Bring her forth without further delay."

"But I already said she isn't here!" Lenore insisted as the prince gestured to the guards, who pushed past into her house. "Stop! What are you doing? You can't barge in here like that!"

"Members of the king's guard can go anywhere the prince commands," said the guard who had pounded on the door. "We know the girl is here; we'll tear your house apart to find her if we must. Make it easier on yourself and bring us the girl now."

"She is not in this house!" said Lenore, looking more frightened than angry.

"The woman was right," Liam said, coming up behind her. "I found the girl shut in a shed behind the house."

He stepped aside, revealing the girl who had danced with the prince the night before. She looked different now with dirt on her ragged clothes and tear streaks through the dust on her face.

"It's all right, dear one," the prince said, taking her hand and leading her to a bench by the door. "All I want you to do is try on this shoe."

"My daughters should be the ones to try on the

shoe," said Lenore, her bony hands on her hips. "This girl is nothing but a servant."

The prince turned to look at her, the expression on his face angry enough to make her take a step back. "This girl is a servant because you made her one," said the prince. "As daughter of the master of the house, she had as much right to be treated well as your own daughters did."

"Perhaps that's true," said Lenore. "But the shoe..."

"Look at your daughters! It's obvious that neither of them is the girl who danced with me last night. Why would I waste my time trying the shoe on them when I know it couldn't possibly be either one?" Turning his back on the woman, the prince took the glass slipper from the cushion and slipped it onto Eleanor's foot with his own hands. The slipper fit perfectly.

Eleanor's eyes were shining when she lifted them to the prince. "I knew it was you," he said, and pulled her to her feet. They stepped closer, and Ainsley bent down until his lips were level with hers. When they kissed, the air around them began to sparkle.

Annie glanced around the room when she heard a sweet melody. She wasn't surprised to see Moonbeam standing in a corner of the room, smiling broadly. "That's it," said the fairy. "They fell in love. My job is done."

"What do you mean, that's it?" asked Annie as

Cinderella and the prince drifted into another room and shut the door. "Love doesn't work that way. You don't meet one day and kiss and see sparkles the next. Real love takes time. They need to get to know each other, and when they do, then they might fall in love. They know next to nothing about each other now."

"I can't believe you're interfering again! Love *can* happen like that. I make it happen all the time." There was a short, sharp rap on the door and Moonbeam turned her head. "Do you hear that?" she asked. "Someone is at the door. I think you need a little lesson. If a man is at the door, you're going to fall in love with him. Open the door," she ordered the guard who was standing closest to it.

"Hey, wait a minute!" said Liam.

"I wouldn't do this if I were you," Annie warned.

Moonbeam wasn't listening. Even as the guard reached for the latch, the fairy was aiming her wand at Annie, saying,

Love can strike
When two first meet
And last forever more.
Make her fall
In love with him
When he walks through the door.

A flood of sparkling lights shot from the wand to Annie, hitting her just above her heart, then bouncing off to splatter all over Moonbeam. The fairy had been laughing, but when her spell bounced back and hit her, she shook her head as if stunned. "What did you do?" she demanded.

"I didn't do anything," Annie told her.

"I've come for my money," the butcher told Lenore, who was staring at Moonbeam. "Your daughter said you'd pay me, but I can't wait until you show up at my shop again. You have to pay me now!"

Moonbeam looked puzzled until she turned and saw the butcher. A flush spread over her cheeks and she began to tremble. "It's you!" she cried. "The man of my dreams!"

The butcher glanced at her, then looked behind him to see who she was talking to, but there was no one there. "Do you mean me?" he asked her, patting himself on the chest. Annie noticed that he had dried blood under his fingernails.

"Yes, I do, you dear man. You're everything I've ever wanted!"

"You wanted a butcher?" he asked, looking puzzled.

"I think we should go," Liam said, coming up behind Annie. "Somehow I don't see this ending well."

"What is your name, my love?" Moonbeam asked the butcher.

"Selbert Dunlop?" he said as if he weren't sure.

"Moonbeam Dunlop," the fairy murmured. "I like the sound of that."

"Moonbeam," said Liam, "about that dwarf..."

"Not now, young man," the fairy said without even looking his way. "I'm talking to my one true love."

"You are?" said Selbert.

"You said you would tell us about the dwarf if we did what you wanted," Annie reminded the fairy. "Just answer our question and we'll leave you alone. Where can we find the dwarf who turned Beldegard into a bear?"

Moonbeam sighed. "I have no idea. I don't know any dwarves who can turn humans into animals."

"Are you sure?" asked Gwendolyn. "Maybe you ran into him during your travels. Short man, beard, raspy voice..."

"Yes, I'm sure!" said Moonbeam. "Now go away and leave us alone!"

Liam scowled and took Annie by the arm. They hadn't even reached the door when he muttered, "I wish she had told us sooner. We wasted a lot of time because of that fairy."

"Where's Gwennie?" Annie asked once they were outside.

"Right here," said her sister, stepping out of the shadows. "Moonbeam told me to wait outside so I wouldn't distract Ainsley."

They were walking away from the house when the door opened again and Moonbeam came out. "You can't go yet!" she called after Annie even as she hurried closer. "First you have to tell me what just happened. Why did my magic bounce off you?"

"Years ago, my mother asked her fairy godmother for help," said Annie. "My parents didn't want a magic christening gift to mess up my life, so the fairy gave me a gift that kept any magic from touching me."

"What idiot would do such a thing?" Moonbeam asked. "Tell me who it was so I can hunt her down and make her wish she'd never seen a magic wand!"

"You really don't remember, do you?" Annie asked. "My mother is Queen Karolina of Treecrest, formerly Princess Karolina of Floradale, and *you* were the fairy who gave me the gift."

CHAPTER 14

BELDEGARD WAS WAITING for them in the woods just beyond the south gate. After he and Gwendolyn had greeted each other, he turned to Liam and said, "So, where do we go next?"

Liam shrugged. "I have no idea. Moonbeam didn't help one bit."

"Why are you asking Liam?" demanded Annie. "Don't you think it's possible that Gwennie or I might have a suggestion?"

"Fine," said the bear prince. "What do *you* suggest?"

"I was dancing with a man at the ball when I mentioned the Dark Forest. He was confused because he thought I was talking about the Black Woods and had the name wrong. What if we did have the name wrong, but in a different way? When Rose Red said the dwarf was from the Black Forest, we thought she meant the Dark Forest, but what if she really meant the Black Woods? Maybe we went to the wrong place."

Gwendolyn nodded. "I bet you're right. Where is the Black Woods, anyway?"

"It's in Montrose," said Beldegard. "A few hours' ride from my parents' castle."

"Lord Camril said that he had met a family of dwarves there once. Yes, Liam, I know that there are bound to be other families of dwarves around," Annie said, holding up her hand when Liam opened his mouth to speak. "But at least there are some dwarves there who we can talk to, and that's more than we've found anywhere else."

"It sounds like as good a place to look as any," said Beldegard. "We'll have to cross the River Rampant and head south."

"Is there a ferry to take us across?" asked Annie.

"There is one farther north," Beldegard told her, "just not anywhere near where we want to go. There might be a bridge we can use, but if there have been storms in the north like we encountered in Farley's Crossing, the river can run high enough to wash out the bridge. If that happens, we'll have to find another way across."

As they shouldered their knapsacks and started off, Annie fell into step beside Liam. "This just keeps getting better and better," she said. "Tell me again why we're doing this."

"So your sister's true love can turn back into a man and she can stop getting a chapped face from bear drool," Liam replied.

"Ah yes," said Annie. "A truly noble cause."

꙾

It was midafternoon when they reached the river and saw a place where there had been a bridge, which was gone. The water was running so high and fast that even Beldegard doubted he could swim across. "I'll see if I can find a boat," the bear prince said, and forced his way into the underbrush at the side of the road.

When Gwendolyn wandered closer to the trees where Beldegard had disappeared, Annie glanced at Liam, who was staring into the turbulent water. "What are you thinking?" she asked, wondering if they might actually be able to talk about why he was being so distant. She'd wanted to talk to him about it before, but Beldegard and Gwendolyn were usually too close and Annie thought it was a conversation that she and Liam should have when they were alone.

"I always keep a hook in my pack in case I have a chance to do a little fishing. I was thinking that I'd like to try my hand now while we wait for Beldegard, but this water is probably too rough." A gull swooped down to skim the surface and came up with something wriggling in its beak. "You know," said Liam, "I think I'll try anyway. I may not catch anything, but it's better than sitting around here twiddling my thumbs. I'll be right back. I just have to cut down a sapling to make a fishing pole."

"He's going to fish?" Gwendolyn asked, joining her sister at the water's edge. "I didn't know that princes knew how."

"Liam is no ordinary prince," Annie told her. "Unlike most princes, he didn't acquire his skills through magic. He taught himself a lot of things because he's interested in a lot of things."

Liam had been gone only a few minutes when they heard shouting and the sound of someone running through the forest. He came back soon after carrying a sapling.

"What happened back there?" Annie asked. "Are you all right?"

"I'm fine," he told her as he started to strip the bark off the sapling. "There was a wolf nosing around, so I chased it off. There's a lot more wildlife in these woods than you'd think. Can you unravel a thread from my blanket while I look for a worm? Maybe I'll get lucky and catch a fish for our dinner."

With Annie's help, Liam soon had the pole assembled. Once he had dropped the baited hook in the water, he sat down with his back against a tree.

"Is that it?" Gwendolyn asked. "I thought it was going to be more dramatic."

"It can be when he actually catches something," said

Annie. "I used to go fishing with the stable boys when you were practicing etiquette and courtly manners. We caught some pretty big fish in the Crystal River."

"I probably won't catch anything today," Liam said. "You might as well sit back and—"

Twang! The line suddenly went taut.

"I've got one!" Liam shouted, giving the pole a quick jerk. When there was still resistance on the line, he yanked the pole back hard and a fish as long as his arm flew out of the water, landing with a *splat* on the ground behind him.

The fish was gasping when Liam bent down to retrieve it, but it wasn't until he picked it up that the fish spoke. "Kind sir, please let me go."

Startled, Liam nearly dropped the fish. "Am I imagining things, or did this fish just talk to me?"

"Of course I spoke," said the fish. "I am a magical fish and will grant you three wishes if you release me back into the water."

"Really?" Liam said. "Any three wishes?"

"Within reason," said the fish.

"Then help us get across the river."

"No," said the fish. "First you have to let me go, *then* I grant you the three wishes. Haven't you noticed that I'm a fish, and I'm out of the water? Toss me back in so I can breathe!"

"Oh, right, sorry!" Liam gently removed the hook from the fish's mouth and set it back in the river.

With a flick of its tail, the fish disappeared into the churning water.

Liam sighed. "So much for my three wishes."

A branch snapped in the forest and Beldegard came bounding onto the road. "I found a boat!" he shouted. "Follow me. It's not far."

"Say," said Liam, his expression brightening. "Maybe I'll get my wishes after all."

"You can ride on my back, my sweet love," Beldegard told Gwendolyn as he came closer. "I don't want the thorns to scratch you."

"Oh, but it's all right if we get scratched," Annie grumbled to Liam.

"If the wishes are really true," Gwendolyn said as she climbed on the bear prince's back, "you should wish for something better, Liam, like we find the dwarf or Beldegard gets turned back into a man now."

"What wishes?" asked the bear prince.

"The fish didn't do anything," said Annie. "I was listening and all I heard was his own personal magic that allows him to talk. The river is noisy, but if the magic was related to you, I should have been able to hear it."

"It's an awfully big coincidence if that's true," said Liam. "I ask for help crossing the river and Beldegard finds a boat we can use."

"That doesn't mean it wasn't a coincidence," said Annie. "Beldegard was looking for a boat anyway."

They argued about the fish's magical abilities as they

struggled through a thicket of thorns, crossed gullies, and climbed jumbled rocks. "You know," Annie finally said, "just because something says it has magic, doesn't mean it really does."

"You're too cynical," said Gwendolyn.

"Maybe," Annie replied, "but you're too trusting."

"I don't know what you're talking about, but here's the boat," said Beldegard, stopping at the edge of the river.

An old dinghy rested on the shore just past the water line. With one snick of his claws, Beldegard snapped the frayed rope that secured the boat to a tree.

"It isn't much of a boat," said Liam as he stepped closer to inspect it.

"Maybe not," the bear prince replied, "but it should do the job." Fitting his shoulder against the side of the boat, he pushed it toward the river. It was almost touching the water when he glanced toward Liam and shouted, "Don't just stand there! Grab the rope!"

Liam lunged and caught the rope just before the boat slid into the river. Water sloshed over the side and Liam shook his head. "I don't know about this..."

"Get in!" Gwendolyn said as she clambered over the side. "This is the answer to your fish wish, remember?"

"What fish?" asked Beldegard.

"Are you swimming across or what?" Liam asked the bear prince.

Beldegard snorted. "In this river? Not likely. This

boat should hold all of us." He hefted himself into the boat, making it tip until Annie thought it was about to capsize. When it had righted itself, it was sitting so low that the water was only inches below the gunnels.

When Annie had taken her seat, Liam pulled the boat as close to the shore as he could get it and stepped in. The boat sank even farther in the water. Taking up the two oars, he slid them into the oarlocks and turned the boat toward the other shore. The current immediately grabbed them and began carrying them downriver, but Liam dipped the oars in the water and, with a few powerful strokes, got it headed in the right direction.

"Well, well, well," said a voice from the water. "So you found a boat. Good for you! Too bad it's going to sink!" They all looked down at the fish swimming beside them. Beldegard growled.

"What do you mean?" asked Liam. "Are you going to make it sink?"

"I don't have to," said the fish. "Look!" A wave washed over the side. Water sloshed around their feet as one wave followed another.

Liam began to row harder. "Can't you help us?" he asked. "I saved your life. I put you back in the water."

"After you took me out! And now I have a sore in my mouth and my throat is scratchy from breathing all that dry air. The last thing I want to do is help you."

"But what about my wishes?" asked Liam. "You said I could have three wishes if I let you go!"

"So I lied!" said the fish. "What are you going to do, catch me again? As if I'd be dumb enough to fall for the old worm floating on the water twice in one day! Besides, if I could do real magic, do you think I'd stay in this lousy river? It's cold enough to freeze off my fins, and half the time it's flooding. Naw, I just want to watch you flounder around in this boat until it sinks. Ha-ha!"

They were halfway across the river now and Liam was struggling with the oars against the current. Annie could see the tendons in his neck stand out each time he dragged the oars back.

"Why don't you just give up?" the fish said to Liam. "You're not going to make it anyway."

"I should never have thrown you back in the water," Liam said, perspiration beading his forehead.

Annie took off her shoe and began to bail the water out of the bottom of the boat; she soon saw that her efforts were doing little. They were nearly three-quarters of the way across, but the waves were growing higher and Liam looked exhausted.

"Is that the fish you were talking about?" said Beldegard, his nose twitching as he sniffed the air.

"That's the one," said Gwendolyn.

"You humans aren't very bright," said the fish. "And bears are even dumber. I bet I know snails that are smarter than you!"

Annie was seated in the front of the boat. The river-bank was so close now that she could almost touch it. "Just a few more feet!" she shouted to Liam.

"I have a question for you," Beldegard said to the fish in a softer voice as he leaned toward the side of the boat.

The fish swam closer, peering up at the bear prince with its cold, round eyes. "Yes?" it said. "What is it?"

"Were you ever a human?"

"Human?" the fish said, sounding incredulous. "Of course not! Now if that isn't the stupidest question I've ever—"

With a swipe of his paw, Beldegard scooped up the fish and shoved it into his mouth. The boat thudded into the riverbank as he closed his eyes and chomped. "That was one obnoxious fish," he said as he climbed out of the boat. "But it certainly was delicious!"

CHAPTER 15

THE CURRENT HAD CARRIED THEM so far downstream that it took them nearly an hour to find their way back to the road. They turned south then and soon found themselves in open country with hay fields on either side.

"Why did you ask the fish if it had ever been human?" Gwendolyn said to Beldegard after a while.

"Because if it had been, I wouldn't have eaten it," said Beldegard.

"It's surprising how many talking animals we've encountered," said Liam. "I wonder how many of them were human once."

"I don't know of any, other than myself and those three bears," the bear prince said, "but then I haven't asked very many."

"That's odd," said Annie.

"Why, it's not like I've had the opportunity—"

Annie shook her head. "No, I mean that little hut over there. I thought it was an extra-big bale of straw until I saw that it had a window and a door."

"Isn't that darling!" Gwendolyn exclaimed. "Do you think someone built it for a child?"

"Out here in the middle of nowhere? I can't imagine who would take the time to ... Gwennie," Annie shouted as her sister started toward the hut. "What are you doing? Come back here!"

"Hello, little guy," Gwendolyn said, peering through the window. "What are you doing in there? Annie, come quick," she called over her shoulder. "There's the cutest little pig in this hut!"

"I live here, lady," the pig said, standing up on his hind legs. "I'm the one who should be asking you questions."

"Did you hear that?" Gwendolyn called to Beldegard. "I found another talking animal!"

The pig leaned out of his window to see her companions. "You have a bear with you?" he asked. "Then you really should go. Prince Maitland has killed off most of the bears in Montrose and is hunting down the last few. He went past this morning and will probably be back any time now."

Gwendolyn's face turned pale. "We have to go somewhere safe!"

"Head for the woods," the pig said, pointing south. "A bear is always safer in the woods."

They walked faster after that, though occasionally one or the other would pause to look behind them. They had almost reached the forest when Beldegard groaned. "I don't feel good," he said. "I don't think that fish agreed with me."

"That fish didn't agree with *anyone*," said Liam. "Can you keep going for now?"

Beldegard grunted and continued on, but Annie could hear his stomach gurgling. She was relieved when they reached the forest, where there were more places for a bear to hide. The shade of the trees felt good as well, although it didn't seem to help Beldegard's noisy stomach.

They had gone only a short distance into the forest when Annie spotted another odd little hut. This one was made entirely of sticks and came only as high as her shoulder. It had a door facing the road and a peaked roof made of leafy twigs. They were walking past when a head appeared in the doorway.

"Look!" Gwendolyn exclaimed. "Another little pig! This one is even more darling than the first."

"We shouldn't stop now," Annie told her sister, who had already started toward the hut.

"I have to lie down," groaned Beldegard.

"Is that a talking bear?" the little pig said, trotting out into the open. "Oh, dear, this isn't good. This isn't good at all! You shouldn't be here, bear. The prince will be by soon and he's determined to rid the kingdom of bears."

"We know," said Annie. "Is there anywhere he can hide?"

"Go deep in the forest, as far from the road as you can," said the little pig. "And hurry! The prince could be along any time!"

Beldegard groaned again. "I don't know if I can walk that far."

"You have to try, my love!" Gwendolyn cried, wringing her hands.

"He just has a stomachache," said Annie. "You don't need to be so dramatic. Come on, Beldegard. We didn't come this far so some prince could take your hide for a trophy."

Liam held a branch aside to let the others pass as they headed into the woods. "We've been in Montrose ever since we crossed the river. If this is your home kingdom, Beldegard, what prince would be out hunting bears?"

"My younger brother, Maitland," panted Beldegard, trudging up a slope with his head hanging low. "I have two sisters, but he's the only other prince, unless it's someone from another kingdom."

"Has your brother always hated bears?" asked Annie.

Beldegard shook his head. "He didn't used to, but he's always loved to hunt." He groaned again and turned to bite at his side. "I don't think I can go any farther."

"If the prince is Beldegard's brother, do we really need to run?" asked Gwendolyn. "We should just tell him who we are and what we're trying to do. I bet Maitland would help us."

"I don't think that's a good idea," said Annie. "Don't you think it's odd that his brother is hunting bears *now*? Until we know what's really going on, I think we should hide Beldegard."

"I agree," said Liam. "Not all siblings are as nice as yours, Gwendolyn. Come on, Beldegard, just a little bit farther. They won't see us once we get over the ridge."

Beldegard's muzzle was nearly touching the ground when he staggered to the top. "This isn't very far from the road," said Gwendolyn, looking back at the woods behind them.

"Keep going," said Liam. "We haven't gone nearly far enough."

Beldegard started down the other side, one slow paw at a time. He'd gone only a few yards when he collapsed.

"Get up, my love," Gwendolyn said, hurrying to his side. "We have to keep moving."

Annie was right behind her sister when she heard a horse whinny. "Someone's on the road!" she said in a loud whisper. "Hurry, we have to hide Beldegard!"

"Where?" Gwendolyn asked, looking around in confusion.

"Here, cover him with this," Annie said, pulling her blanket from her knapsack. The bear prince had collapsed in a slight depression in the ground, which his bulk more than filled. Annie was glad that there wasn't more of him to cover, as her blanket was barely big enough. It was a dull brown, not too different from the forest floor, and when they scattered leaves across its surface, Beldegard was almost impossible to see.

"They're coming this way," said Liam from the top of the ridge. "Sit down and act natural. Pretend we just stopped for a bite to eat. Gwendolyn, stop looking like the world is about to end. Take something out of your bag and eat it!"

Gwendolyn looked as frightened as a fawn in a dragon's den. "I don't think this is the time—" she began.

"Ooh," groaned Beldegard.

"Gwendolyn, sit by his head and keep him quiet!" Liam told her as he hurried to join them.

While Gwendolyn carefully took a seat at one end of Beldegard, Annie plopped down next to his stomach and opened her knapsack, setting it on him as if he were a bump in the ground. She had just taken the first bite of hard cheese when five men on horseback appeared over the ridge.

"Good day!" Liam said, getting to his feet.

Annie noticed that he kept his hand near his sword; she wondered what he'd do if the men proved to be dangerous. Five armed men against one were not very good odds.

"Good day," replied the young man who seemed to be leader of the group. Well dressed and with wavy brown hair, he looked a lot like Beldegard did whenever Annie's touch made him turn back into a human. "My men and I are bear hunting. A particularly nasty one has been ravaging these woods of late. I would be careful if I were you."

"Thank you for the warning," Liam said. "And you are..."

"Prince Maitland," said the young man. "Heir to the throne of Montrose."

"I thought Prince Beldegard was the heir to the throne," Gwendolyn said.

Maitland turned to face her. "He was," he said, and shook his head as if in great sorrow. "He died on a quest two years ago. And who, may I ask, are you?"

"Just some travelers," said Liam.

"*You* may be," said Prince Maitland, "but this lovely lady is not." With one fluid motion, he threw his leg over his horse and dismounted. Gwendolyn didn't move when the prince strode to her side and pulled her hood back from her face and her cap off her hair.

The mounted riders stirred, their horses responding by shifting their feet. Liam took a step closer, but

Annie caught his eye and shook her head. One thing Gwendolyn knew how to do was deal with men.

"How did you know I was a lady?" Gwendolyn asked, looking up at him through her eyelashes.

"Your voice, your hands, a hint of your cheek. Who are you, my lady? You are the most beautiful woman I have ever seen!"

"My name is Gwendolyn," she said.

Once again the men stirred, but this time because their prince had fallen to his knees at her feet. "Princess Gwendolyn! The most beautiful princess in all the kingdoms! What are you doing here, my lady?" he asked, taking her hands in his and holding them as if they were fragile birds that might fly away.

"I am on a most urgent and secret quest, my kind prince. One that I must complete with my two companions before I can marry my true love."

"And who may this true love of yours be?" the prince asked, his eyes darkening.

"I have yet to see his real face," said Gwendolyn.

"You mean there might yet be hope…"

"There is always hope, dear prince," she told him, giving him the same sweet smile Annie had seen her practice in mirrors countless times. "You must leave us now so we might continue our quest."

"And I'll see you again once you've completed it?" asked Prince Maitland.

"I'm sure of that," Gwendolyn told him.

The prince raised her hand to his lips. After releasing her, he stood and took a step back. "Then we'll be off," he said, and gestured to his men.

No one moved while the prince and his men rode away. When he stopped at the top of the ridge to wave to Gwendolyn, she waved to him, then continued to watch as he disappeared over the other side.

"Wow!" Annie said, shaking her head in amazement. "You handled that really well."

"I know," Gwendolyn said with a smug smile.

"I thought he was about to declare his undying love for you," said Annie. "And when you said you had to go on an urgent and secret quest so you could marry your true love, that was inspired! He thought you might be talking about him, didn't he?"

"Maybe," Gwendolyn said, looking coy.

"Well, I didn't like it," Beldegard said, getting to his feet so that the blanket, leaves, and Annie's knapsack slid off and she had to scramble out of the way. Annie had been so close to him that he now looked mostly human. "What were you doing, flirting with my brother?" he asked Gwendolyn. "I noticed you didn't tell him that you *have* a true love."

"I wasn't flirting with him! I mean I was, but not like you think!" said Gwendolyn. "I was trying to get him to go away and leave us alone. And what was I supposed to do, tell him that I intend to marry his brother, the bear, when everyone seems to think that telling him who you are is a very bad idea. And why is that, anyway?" she said, whirling around to face Annie.

"It may not be," Annie said, shrugging. "But it's better to be safe than sorry. I just think it was a little too much of a coincidence that Beldegard is a bear and his younger brother is out hunting bears when we just happen to be passing through the kingdom. If I'm not mistaken, if Beldegard were to die, Prince Maitland would be the one to inherit the throne."

"That's true," said the bear prince, who was looking more bearlike by the moment. "But Maitland has never been interested in the throne. He's always been more interested in hunting and having parties with his friends."

"That may be so, but I think he's interested in the throne now!" said Annie. "He *is* introducing himself as the heir."

"How would he know I'm a bear?" asked Beldegard.

Annie shook her head. "Are you kidding me? Nearly two weeks ago, half the princes in the kingdoms learned who you were. I'm sure word has traveled all over by now."

"You sound a lot better, Beldegard," said Liam. "Are you feeling all right?"

The bear prince grunted. "I started feeling better when Annie leaned against my stomach. I think she took away the fish's magic long enough that I could start digesting it. I feel great now, or I *would* if I hadn't heard what I heard," he said, turning to give Gwendolyn an injured look.

"But Beldegard, you know I love *you!*" she cried.

"Haven't seen his real face, huh? What do you suppose this is?" the bear prince said, patting his cheek with his paw.

"That's the face the dwarf's magic gave you!" she cried, running to catch up as he stalked off. "You know I've never seen your real face, not even when Annie holds your hand. You still look a little bearlike then and I..."

"I don't know which is worse, being around them when they've all lovey-dovey or when they're arguing," said Annie.

"I think listening to Gwendolyn talk to Beldegard's brother was the worst," said Liam. "But she did seem to know what she was doing."

CHAPTER 16

ANNIE GLANCED FROM BELDEGARD to Gwendolyn. Neither one had spoken to the other for the entire afternoon. When Annie refused to get drawn into a conversation with her sister about Beldegard, Gwennie had stopped talking to her as well. It was getting dark now and past the time when they should have started looking for somewhere to spend the night, but no one had brought it up yet.

"Quiet!" Beldegard growled, although no one had said anything. "Listen!" he added in a whisper.

Annie closed her eyes and listened, but all she could hear were the usual sounds of dusk. The occasional bird sang good night to its neighbors as they settled down to sleep; an angry squirrel chattered somewhere in the forest while leaves rustled overhead, sounding like the rush of water. And then it came again, the whinny of a horse calling to other horses.

"Have you heard it before?" Liam asked the bear prince.

Beldegard nodded. "Off and on all day. They've been following us, but keeping their distance."

"Do you think it's Maitland and his men?" asked Annie.

"More than likely," said Beldegard. "But there isn't much we can do about it."

Annie was confused. "Why do you think he's staying back and not confronting Beldegard now?"

"Probably because he'd have too many witnesses if he attacked his brother in front of us," said Liam. "It would be a lot easier for him to deny that he knew it was Beldegard if Gwendolyn wasn't there to shout, 'That's my true love! Don't hurt him!' I think he's waiting until he can catch Beldegard alone in the woods hunting for food or until it's dark."

"That's simple then," said Annie. "Don't go anywhere without us, Beldegard."

"I'm not going to let him out of my sight, even if he is being thickheaded," Gwendolyn said. "Do you think we can stop for the night soon? My feet are killing me!"

"We'll stop as soon as we can find someplace safe to sleep," Liam told her.

They continued on as the light faded, looking for a likely place to make camp. At one point Liam spotted something moving between the trees. When he threw a stick at it, the animal ran off. "Another wolf," he said as if it were nothing, but Annie noticed that he kept his hand on his scabbard and stopped now and then to look back behind them.

It was Annie who spotted a flicker of light in the woods. At first she thought it might be fairies, but when it stayed in one place rather than dart from tree to tree, she touched Liam's sleeve and pointed. "Is that a fire burning back there?"

Liam peered into the woods. "I think it's a cottage," he said after a moment. "Beldegard, Annie might have found a place for us to stay."

They walked single file behind Beldegard with Liam in the back. As they drew closer, Annie could see that the light was coming from a cottage window and that whoever was inside was throwing a party. Loud voices shouted, while others sang a drinking song. Figures moved past the window, their bodies blocking the light to create dancing silhouettes.

When they were close enough to see the entire cabin, Annie noticed something odd. "Look there," she told her friends. "By the back. There's a figure standing outside a window, watching the people at the party."

"I see him," said Beldegard. "Let me look around before you go any closer."

Beldegard was padding toward the cottage when the figure slunk away from the window. Suddenly the door slammed open, there was a terrible racket, and the candles went out, leaving only the dim glow from a fire in the fireplace. Men poured from the cottage, tearing down the path.

Annie and her friends stepped out of their way as the men raced by. They were a rough group, their faces weather-worn and scarred. Even in the near dark, Annie could see the whites of eyes wide in terror.

"Who could scare those men like that?" Annie whispered to Liam.

"I don't know," said Liam. "Something strange is going on and I'm not waiting for Beldegard to see what it is."

Annie and Gwendolyn followed Liam to the window and peered inside. It was a one-room cottage with a fireplace in the back. In the center of the room stood a table covered with a red tablecloth and piled high with food. A roast goose rested on a golden platter beside a tureen of still-steaming soup. Bowls of potatoes, stewed greens, carrots, squash, and corn vied for space on the table with a glistening ham, grilled fish, fruit pies, wheels of cheese, loaves of bread, and a cake shaped like a castle. Annie's mouth watered at the aromas wafting from the cottage. Gwendolyn made a whimpering sound.

Suddenly a gray-and-white-striped cat jumped onto the table and began to devour the fish. Then a rooster landed in the bowl of corn and began pecking. A moment later a scruffy white dog set her front paws on the table and pulled the ham off the platter while a donkey trotted to the far end and buried his face in an apple pie.

Still watching through the window with Gwennie, Annie wasn't the only one who was startled when Beldegard bounded into the cottage looking fierce. The rooster flew into the rafters while the dog, the cat, and the donkey shrank back.

Swinging his great head around, the bear prince sniffed the air and growled, "Where is he?"

The cat and the dog glanced at each other, then the dog sat down on her haunches, tilted her head to the side, and said, "Who?"

"The person who scared those men off," said Beldegard.

The dog stared at the prince. "The person? Oh, you mean..." When she opened her mouth again, her tongue lolled to the side, the curled tip bouncing with each breath. The cat's lips pulled back, almost as if he was smiling, the rooster hopped from one foot to the other, and the donkey brayed loud and long. Annie suspected that the animals were laughing.

"That wasn't a man," said the cat. "That was us!"

Beldegard shook his head. "I saw him. It was a tall, lumpy man."

"That *was* us!" said the donkey. "See!" Striding to the middle of the room, the donkey planted his feet and held his head high. In two bounds, the dog jumped onto the donkey's back. As the rooster fluttered down to land on the donkey's head, the cat jumped from the table to the back of the dog. When they were all settled, the donkey began to bray, the dog to bark, the cat to yowl, and the rooster to crow. It was the same awful sound she had heard when the figure scared the men from the cottage.

"Very impressive," said Beldegard. "But why did you want to scare them away?"

"They were thieves," said the cat. "They stole our master's magic tablecloth that brings food when you want it. We deserve the tablecloth more than they do."

As the cat and dog jumped down from the donkey's back, the rooster flew to the table and began to peck at a loaf of bread. "Would you mind if my friends and I come inside?" asked Beldegard. "We're hungry as well and the night is cold. I promise you, we're not thieves and will not steal your magic tablecloth. We just need a place to spend the night and will leave in the morning."

"Come on in," said the dog. "There's lots of food. If we run out, the tablecloth can always bring more."

Liam, Gwendolyn, and Annie had heard everything the animals had said, so they didn't wait for an invitation. When the cat saw them in the doorway, she gave Beldegard an accusing look. "You didn't say your friends are human! Ah well, we won't hold that against them. Shut the door and help yourselves to the food. I wouldn't eat the ham, though. Dog has mangled it so no one else will want any."

The dog hung her head and put her tail between her legs. "Sorry."

Annie was too hungry to care about a few animals on the table. She made herself a trencher with a hollowed-out slab of bread and filled it with goose and vegetables and everything else that she thought looked tempting.

She took her food to a bed that stood against the wall and sat down to eat. Gwendolyn joined her a minute later and sat close enough that her beauty began to fade. Liam sat down on the other side of Annie and soon the only sound in the room was that of the donkey munching carrots and the dog slurping soup from the tureen.

"Where are you from?" Beldegard asked the cat after finishing off the fish and a berry pie.

"Brementown, originally, but lately we've been making our home in Grelia," said the cat. "We lived there with our master until he died a few days ago. He was a wizard and used his magic to make us speak so we could be his servants. I was with him for fourteen years, but he was already old when I was just a kitten, and his health had never been good. The thieves came when word got out that he'd died, and they took most of his possessions. We followed them through the woods to this cottage. It isn't right that they should have the old wizard's things."

"We couldn't stay in the wizard's house in the city," said the rooster, his voice hoarse from crowing. "We're all old. No one wants us anymore."

"That's not quite true," said the cat. "We heard our master's neighbors talking. One of them was going to take Rooster for the stew pot."

"And one wanted me for my hide," the donkey told the bear prince.

The dog looked up from the ham bone she was gnawing. "I know who you are. You're Beldegard."

"How did you know that?" the bear prince asked.

The dog dropped the bone long enough to say, "People talk. I listen. They say in the capital that Beldegard was turned into a bear. You talk like a prince. You must be him."

"Was this a widespread rumor?" asked Annie. "Were a lot of people saying it?"

The rooster nodded, making his red crest bob up and down. "Everybody."

"That settles it then," said Annie. "If it was common knowledge, your brother Maitland had to know, too, Beldegard. He must want the throne."

Beldegard growled and swatted at the table, knocking a mincemeat pie onto the floor. The dog sauntered over to sniff it. "My belly is so full I couldn't eat a pea, but it would be a shame to waste this," the dog said, and began gobbling up the broken pie.

Gwendolyn set her trencher on the table and hurried to the bear prince's side. "Oh Beldegard," she said, throwing her arms around his neck. "I'm so sorry! Your brother may no longer love you, but you'll always have me!"

Beldegard nuzzled her shoulder and said something into her ear.

"I guess their argument is over," Liam told Annie.

Annie nodded. "I'm surprised it lasted as long as it did. You know, I've been thinking. When we met Maitland in the forest, I think he suspected who Gwennie was before he pulled down her hood. We had attended the ball the day before and I'm sure a lot of people were talking about her. I bet people saw us leave the city too, and noted which way we went. If Maitland knew about Gwennie, do you think he knew that she was traveling with Beldegard?"

"Not necessarily," said Liam. "Beldegard has been careful to stay out of sight when we run into other people."

"Except when we were talking to Rose Red, and those men went after him with pitchforks. A lot of people saw him with Gwennie then. And that was back before she started wearing the hood. Besides, everyone knows that his kiss ended the curse. It makes sense that she'd be helping him now."

"So Beldegard," said the cat. "I heard people say you were turned into a bear, but I never heard anyone say how it happened. Did you get a witch angry or was it a fairy?"

"Neither," grumbled the bear. "It was a dwarf. I was on a quest when I heard that a dragon had carried off a princess. Her father was offering her hand in marriage to the brave man who rescued her. I slayed the dragon, but the princess ran off with one of her father's knights before our wedding day. Her father was furious, and so embarrassed that he gave me a chest full of jewels. I was on my way home with my treasure when the dwarf waylaid me and turned me into a bear."

"Oh, Beldy, I knew you were brave!" cried Gwendolyn. "But I didn't know you'd slayed a dragon! There are so many things I don't know about you."

"That's all right, my dearest. After we're wed, we'll have a lifetime to learn everything there is to know about each other."

"My stomach is churning," Liam murmured.

Annie frowned at him. "I think what he said was very sweet. It wouldn't hurt you to say something like that once in a while."

"Really?" Liam said. "You like that kind of thing?"

"Most girls do," replied Annie. When he looked puzzled, she sighed and said, "I'm going to sleep now. Good night, everyone."

Annie stretched out on the bed with her back to the room. She didn't go to sleep right away, but lay listening to her companions as they found their own places to rest. The bed moved as Gwendolyn lay down with her back to Annie's. She heard Liam mutter to himself as he made his bed out of a blanket on the floor near the fireplace.

Annie couldn't understand Liam. He could be so sweet sometimes. But he never had finished what he'd started to say in the Gasping Guppy, and whenever Beldegard said something sweet to Gwennie, Liam had made fun of him. After Prince Ainsley's ball, Annie had been sure that Liam really cared for her, but he still always seemed to back off without really telling her so. He hadn't kissed her in days and she missed it; she just didn't know how to tell him. Remembering their last kiss, she touched her lips with a fingertip. If only he would kiss her again!

৵

Annie moved her legs aside when the cat jumped onto the bed, giving him enough room to curl up in a soft, warm ball by her feet. She thought she'd never fall asleep with the donkey snoring loudly in the corner, but her sister warmed her back and the cat snuggled against her feet, so she soon drifted off. It seemed like only moments later that she woke to the cat poking her face with his paw.

"The thieves are back! I can hear them," growled the dog.

Annie sat up and looked around the room. Although it was still dark, enough starlight came through the window that she could see vague outlines. Gwendolyn was asleep, but the animals were all awake, watching the door. Liam stood by the hearth with his sword in his hand and Beldegard was on his feet, rubbing his back against the edge of the stone fireplace; both had their eyes on the door.

The door was creaking open when Annie turned her head. She held her breath as two ... four ... six men crept into the cottage, each carrying a weapon that glinted red in the light of the fireplace. The last man had just stepped over the threshold when the rooster launched himself from the rafter, crowing as he landed on the head of one of the thieves.

Gwendolyn woke with a start and looked around, confused.

The rooster began to peck at one man who screamed and tried to fend off the bird. By then the dog had dashed across the room and bitten a second thief and the cat launched himself onto the shoulders of another man, biting and clawing.

"The monster is still here!" cried the first man.

"Run!" shouted the second.

Beldegard rose up on his hind legs. His head brushed the bottom of the rafters as he stomped toward the door, casting a fearsome, wavering shadow across the room. Throwing back his head, Beldegard ROARED so that the cottage shook, the men screamed, and Annie and Gwendolyn covered their ears.

The men were fighting to get out when the donkey turned so that his tail was toward the door and began to kick with his hind legs. Squeezing through the doorway two and three at a time, the thieves piled out of the cottage and ran as fast as they could.

Beldegard roared one last time, then settled down on all fours.

"That worked well!" he said.

The dog ran to the doorway and peered out into the dark. "They're still running."

"I don't think they'll ever come back," the cat said as he hopped onto the bed again.

"Good!" said the donkey. "Now maybe we can get some sleep!"

CHAPTER 17

THE ROOSTER CROWED at dawn the next morning, startling everyone awake.

"Does he do this every morning?" asked Annie.

The dog sat up and started scratching her ear with her back foot. "Always."

"Then I'm glad he's not traveling with us," grumbled Gwendolyn.

After a hearty breakfast provided by the tablecloth, Annie and her companions prepared to leave. Liam and Beldegard had already gone outside when the cat said to Annie, "Last night when the thieves came back I tried to talk to you, but I couldn't speak. I could talk again when I was no longer near you. Why is that?"

"Magic doesn't work around me," Annie told him.

"I thought it was something like that," said the cat. "So as long as I keep my distance, I should still be able to talk?"

"That's right."

"Good to know," said the cat. "My friends and I want to go with you. We can be very helpful," he said when Annie and Gwendolyn looked reluctant.

"I can carry you on my back," offered the donkey.

"I can bark at strangers," said the dog.

"I can catch the mice before they eat your food," promised the cat.

"And I'll wake you every morning at dawn," added the rooster.

Annie winced. "We could have done without that last offer. How about we let you come as long as the rooster *doesn't* wake us every morning at dawn?"

"Sure, if that's what you want," the cat said, looking at her as if she were crazy.

The donkey was the first animal out the door. He was waiting for them when the sisters emerged from the cottage. "Who wants a ride?" he asked.

Liam gave Annie a quizzical look. She shrugged and said, "They want to come with us. Do you mind?"

"Not at all," he said. The dog thumped her tail.

When the donkey moved closer, Liam and the princesses looked him over. He was an old creature with a sagging back and a patchy coat. His mane was thin in places and none of him was very clean. Because he had no saddle, whoever rode him would have to ride bareback.

"I think Gwendolyn should go first," Annie said,

even as her sister was saying the same about her. "You're older than I am," Annie told her. "And you said that your feet hurt last night."

"I'll help you up," Liam said.

Gwendolyn gave both Liam and Annie dirty looks as she climbed onto the donkey's back. "I won't forget this," Gwendolyn told her sister.

Annie just smiled and turned to the cat. "Do you four have names?" she asked as the donkey began to walk. Gwendolyn squealed and almost fell off, but she regained her balance and grabbed hold of the donkey's meager mane.

"Of course we have names," said the cat. "Our master gave them to us. I'm Cat, and the dog is Dog, and the rooster is Rooster."

"Let me guess," said Liam. "The donkey is named Donkey."

The donkey snorted. "Don't be silly. My name is Quentin. No one names a donkey Donkey!"

"Master had a friend named Quentin who he said was a real donkey," Cat announced. "He thought they should have the same name."

❧

They had gone only a few miles when they entered an older forest that Beldegard said had to be the Black Woods. The trees were taller, making the shade deeper even on a cloudless day. It was quieter than most forests as well, almost as if the songbirds and other forest creatures were afraid to venture there. The silence soon wore on Annie's nerves and she found herself glancing behind her and peering into the gloom, afraid of what she might see.

The forest must have made Gwendolyn nervous as well, because she began talking in a bright cheerful voice as if to make up for the silence. She was telling Beldegard what she wanted to wear for their wedding when the sound of hammering made her stop midsentence and she urged Quentin closer to the bear prince. A few minutes later they heard voices.

"I told you not to make the chimney big! It's supposed to draw the smoke out of the fireplace, not let a wandering dragon or flock of eagles swoop in for a friendly visit!"

"We couldn't help it!" replied a voice Annie had heard before. "We were trying to get the bricks lined up right and we got a little carried away. Neither of us ever claimed we were masons. Enrique and I are just trying to be helpful. If you aren't satisfied with our work, you should do it all yourself. You're the only one who knows how to lay a straight line of bricks."

"If we're to get this cottage done quickly, I can't do everything myself. You know I had to finish the walls. If I didn't get them just right, the whole thing could fall down. Ah well, what's done is done," said the first voice as Annie and her companions rounded a curve in the road. "It will have to do for now."

"Look!" said Gwendolyn. "It's the little pigs! And they have another pig with them."

Three pigs stood by the side of the road, eyeing a tidy little house made of red brick with a yellow tile roof. Bigger than either the house made of straw or the house made of twigs, it was almost as big as a house made for humans. Its chimney, however, was huge, and would have been more appropriate for a much bigger house.

"Don't look now," one of the pigs whispered in a loud voice to the others, "but I think those people are staring at us."

"I met them before," said the smallest pig. Annie recognized him as the one who had built the house of twigs.

"I met them, too," said the middle-size pig, who had built the house of straw.

"Then I guess it's my turn to meet them," said the largest pig. "Hello!" he said, walking on his hind legs to the road where Annie and her friends were watching. "My name is Curcio. I understand you've already met my brothers, Enrique and Anselmo."

"Indeed we have," said Liam.

"Would you like to come inside for some tea?" asked Curcio. "I'm just about to brew a fresh pot."

"You go ahead," said Beldegard. "If I go in there no

one else would fit. I'll scout around and see what I can find."

"But Maitland...," Gwendolyn began.

"If my brother is following us, I'll be going away from him, not toward him. Don't worry, I'll be fine. I won't go far and I'll be back soon."

"You'd better," said Gwendolyn, ruffling the fur on the top of his head. "You know how much I miss you when we're apart."

"We'll stay out here," said Cat as Quentin and the other animals wandered off. "I hear mice in the woodpile."

Liam was the first one through the cottage door. It was a sturdy structure, with a large room in the front and two smaller rooms in the back. The windows were only as wide as one brick was long—just enough to let air and a little light into the cottage. The fireplace in the larger room was as big as the chimney implied, with an opening almost tall enough for Annie to stand in. But the ceilings were so low that Liam had to walk bent over.

"This is charming!" Gwendolyn said, following them into the room. She ran her hand across the child-sized oak table that stood in front of the fireplace.

"I whipped that table up last night," said the pig named Anselmo. "I was a carpenter before *he* came along."

"Who is *he*?" asked Annie.

199

"The dwarf who turned us into pigs," said Curcio. "Please be seated and I'll tell you what happened while I start the water for the tea. Would you mind locking the door? A wolf has been terrorizing my brothers and we're afraid he might come here."

"A wolf?" Liam asked as he slid the bolt that locked the door.

Enrique nodded. "He came to my cottage not five minutes after you did. I ran inside and locked the door when I saw him, so he stood in my yard and threatened me. When I refused to go out, he huffed and puffed and blew my beautiful little house of straw down. Fortunately, I'd already escaped out the back door and hid in the hay behind my house. I used to be a farmer, you see, and that was one of my fields."

As the little pig talked, Annie took a seat on the low bench that ran the length of the table. Gwendolyn sat on the other bench, wincing when she bumped her knees. After eyeing the benches, Liam sat cross-legged on the floor beside Annie. They all watched Curcio add a log to the already burning fire.

"You had already gone by and so had the prince and his men when the wolf came to my house," said Anselmo. "I was looking out my door when I saw him, so I slammed it shut and locked it just before he tried to barge in. He started shouting threats at me, trying to make me come out, but when I didn't he huffed and he puffed and he blew my beautiful little house of twigs down.

I'd already run out the back door and was hiding in the woods behind my cottage."

"My brothers came to stay with me after that," said Curcio, "and have been helping me build my beautiful house of bricks. I was a mason and built many of the better houses here in the Black Woods, although you wouldn't know I could do such fine work if you look at the chimney on this house. I appreciate my brothers' help, but such shoddy work is embarrassing!"

"It's not that bad!" grumbled Anselmo.

"I've known a wolf was following us," Liam said. "But tell us more about this dwarf who turned you into pigs."

"He was a nasty piece of work," said the little pig. "Enrique and I were visiting our brother, when the dwarf walked into the farmhouse as if he owned it. What was it—a week ago?" he asked his brothers.

"Something like that," replied Enrique. "The days all blend together now."

"And you say it was just one dwarf? There wasn't an older one with him?"

Curcio shook his head as he set a pot of water on a hook over the fire. "There was just the one. 'I'm hungry,' the dwarf said. 'Bring me a pitcher of ale and a haunch of venison.'"

"'This isn't an inn,' I told him," said Enrique. "'Get out of my house. You have no right to be here.'"

"But the dwarf just laughed," said Anselmo. "So I

picked him up—I was a big man then—and carried him to the door. He got all red-faced and angry and told me to take my hands off him. He called me a pig, then he really began to laugh. The next thing I knew, I was a little pig, and so were my brothers. One of my neighbors kicked us out of the house the next day and moved his own family in. 'This house is much too good for pigs,' he said."

"Here we go," said Curcio, deftly lifting the pot from the fire. He used his two front trotters to hold the pot steady as he poured the boiling water into earthenware mugs.

"A dwarf turned my true love Beldegard into a bear," said Gwendolyn. "It has to be the same dwarf. We're looking for him now so he can turn Beldegard back."

"How are you going to find him?" asked Curcio.

"We've been told that he was called home to the Black Woods because of a family emergency," said Annie. She turned to Liam to say, "He and his brother must have split up before they got this far."

"His family lives here in the Black Woods?" Curcio said. "I know where a family of dwarves lives. I rebuilt their chimney for them about five years ago when a storm knocked their old one down. I can tell you how to—"

The door handle rattled, making everyone turn around. "Little pig! Little pig! Let me come in!" cried a scratchy voice.

"It's that wolf!" cried Anselmo. "Are you sure the door is locked?"

"I'm sure," said Liam.

"Little pig! Little pig! I won't go away. I just want to hear what you have to say!"

"He means he just wants to eat us," said Enrique.

"We're not letting you in, no matter how much you lie!" Curcio yelled at the door.

"Then I'll huff and I'll puff and I'll blow your house down!" cried the wolf.

Liam jumped to his feet, but he forgot that the ceiling was low and bumped his head against it. He was rubbing his head with one hand when he set his other hand on the hilt of his sword.

Anselmo fidgeted, too nervous to stand still. "I knew he'd be here sooner or later," he said.

Enrique began to nibble the edge of one of his front trotters, his eyes glued to the door.

Curcio ran to a window slit and peered out. "I can't see a thing," he told them as he moved on to the next. "I made these windows narrow so nothing can get in, but I can't see much through them. I should have put more of the blasted things in this wall. Oh, wait, there he is. Yup, he's blowing at the house."

The sound of coughing came from outside. "It looks like he's giving up now," said the pig, peering out of the window again. "He's walking away. I think we should stay inside for a while, just to make sure. I'll heat up more water. We might as well have another cup of tea." The little pig was setting the pot on the fireplace hook when there was a thump on the roof and the sound of scrabbling claws on the tile.

"He's on the roof!" Anselmo said, staring at the ceiling.

Suddenly dust poofed out of the chimney into the room. There was a scratching, clawing, whooshing sound and the wolf fell out of the chimney into the room, knocking the pot of water off its hook and dousing the fire.

"Ow!" he howled, scrambling to get out of the fireplace. "Those coals are hot!"

The wolf lurched into the room and skidded to a stop when he saw that the tip of Liam's sword was only inches from his long, pointy nose. "That was a bad idea, Wolf," Liam said, taking a step closer. "I've skewered many wolves before, but never one who can speak."

"There's no need to be violent," said the wolf, backing away. "I just wanted to talk to the little porkers."

"Really?" said Annie. "And do you always drool when you want to talk to someone?"

"I can't help it! They smell really good and I haven't eaten in a while. But I didn't come here to eat them. I just wanted to ask them something. Would you mind putting that sword down?" he asked Liam.

"Yes, I would mind. Go ahead and ask your question before my patience deserts me," Liam replied.

"It's just that they don't act like pigs, so I was wondering if they were humans once, before a certain dwarf came by—"

"He must have overheard us talking," said Annie. "That's how he knows about the dwarf. I don't trust him. He hasn't stopped drooling since he got here."

"I told you I was hungry. I can't control it. I can't control a lot of things since the dwarf changed me. I don't know the first thing about being a wolf."

"Aren't you the one who scared Little Red Riding Hood's grandmother out of her house?" asked Gwendolyn.

"Hey, at least I didn't eat her! I was starving and no one was going to give me food if I just went up and asked. When I saw Little Red carrying a basket of food I thought she could help me."

"If you were so hungry, why didn't you chase down a rabbit or something?" asked Gwendolyn.

"You people don't listen very well. I told you, I don't know how to be a wolf. My body wants me to eat raw meat, but I still find it revolting. The dwarf turned me into a wolf just last week and I've been eating people food whenever I can."

"If that's true, how did the dwarf turn you into a wolf?" asked Liam.

The wolf sighed. "I was in a tavern, minding my own business playing cards with my friends, when the dwarf insisted on joining us. We hadn't played more than a few hands when he accused me of cheating. The next thing you know, I'm scratching fleas with my back foot and men with pitchforks are coming after me. Running away wasn't easy 'cause I had no idea how to do it with four feet."

"So you're saying you really were a human?" asked Gwendolyn.

"All my life, until the day I met that dwarf. My name is Yardley."

"Wasn't that the name of Rose Red's boyfriend?" Annie said.

"You know Rosey?" said the wolf. "I felt bad for running off like I did, but I didn't want her to see me this way."

Liam scowled at the wolf. "So you've come all the way from Treecrest. And you wanted to talk to the pigs because..."

"I wanted to know about the dwarf and no one else would talk to me! I would have talked to you after I heard you say you were looking for him, but it didn't seem like the right time with Little Red's uncle standing there with an ax in his hand. And then every time I tried to get close enough to have a conversation you chased me off," the wolf said, giving Liam an accusing look. "Where is the bear, anyway? I thought you had all gone ahead when I saw his prints heading down the road."

"He'll be back soon," said Gwendolyn.

"Listen, if you're looking for that dwarf, maybe I should go with you. I can help track him, or hold him down while you make him undo his magic. I could gnaw on him some, too. I wouldn't like it," the wolf said when he saw the horrified look on Annie's face, "but it might make him easier to convince."

"Do you know what the dwarf smells like?" Liam asked.

"Not really. I didn't learn how to use my sniffer until I'd been running for a few days."

"Then how can you track him?" asked Annie.

"I could ... I mean maybe if I ... I guess I couldn't, but then there are other things I could do. Like scare off that prince who's been following you. He sure seems to have it in for that bear friend of yours. All the prince talks about is what he's going to do with the bear's hide."

"I guess Prince Maitland didn't give up," said Liam. "Listen, Wolf. If you really want to help, why don't you distract the prince? I doubt you'd be able to scare him off, but it would help if you could keep him from following too closely. We don't need him coming after Beldegard when we're so near to finding the dwarf. Do you think you could do that?"

"And stay away from the little pigs," said Annie. "They were humans once, too."

"If it would help you get the dwarf, I'd distract a dozen princes," the wolf said, giving them a lopsided grin.

"One will be enough," said Annie. "The rest of the princes around here have a job to do."

CHAPTER 18

"DO YOU TRUST HIM?" Annie asked Liam as they left the pigs' cottage behind.

"Who, the wolf? I know his type. He'll help us as long as he thinks it benefits him. He wants Beldegard to convince the dwarf to undo his magic, so he probably will try to keep Prince Maitland away. As for the pigs—I'm not sure I believe that he's fighting his wolfly urges to kill for meat, so before we left I suggested that Curcio and his brothers stay inside for a while. He said he's going to block off half the chimney to keep intruders out."

"Do you remember the directions he gave to the dwarves' cottage? They sounded fairly complicated."

"No problem," said Liam. "Go past the lake, then turn left at the fork in the road. Go right at the next fork, then left, then look for the cottage with the well-built chimney."

"Sounds like this road has more forks than our old master's chest of silverware," said the cat from atop the donkey's back. Neither Annie nor Gwendolyn wanted to ride that day, so the cat and the rooster were riding instead.

Beldegard grunted. "Unless I'm mistaken, we'll have crossed the border between Montrose and Helmswood before we reach the cottage."

"Do you think Maitland will follow us across the border?" asked Gwendolyn.

"He will if he really wants to get rid of me," Beldegard replied. "My brother isn't known for giving up easily."

❧

By the time they reached the last turn, the road was little more than a path winding between the towering trees. Annie was sure they'd found the right cottage when she saw the chimney that looked like a narrower version of the little pigs'.

An old woman pushing a cart was walking away as Annie and her companions approached the cottage. The woman's shoulders were shaking, but because Annie could see only her back, she couldn't tell if the woman was laughing or crying. For a moment, Annie heard a thin, high-pitched hum that she knew meant evil magic. Then the woman disappeared among the trees, Liam knocked on the door, and a lilting voice sang out, "Just a moment!" from inside the cottage.

When the door opened, instead of a dwarf, a lovely young girl with black hair and fair skin stood inside. "Oh!" she said, looking surprised when she saw them. "I thought the old woman had come back. We don't usually get so many visitors."

The high-pitched hum was louder now and seemed to be coming from the girl. Suddenly her eyes looked frantic and she began to clutch at the ruby necklace around her throat. Her red lips were turning blue when Annie realized what was happening.

"She's choking!" Annie exclaimed, pushing Liam aside. "The necklace is strangling her!"

Even as she reached for it, Annie could see that the necklace was biting into the soft white flesh of the girl's neck. The girl was gasping for air when Annie grabbed hold of the necklace. The moment she touched it, the necklace stopped shrinking and relaxed until it was back to its original size. The hum stopped then as well, and didn't resume even after Annie had undone the clasp and tossed the necklace out the door into the forest.

"The old woman just sold that to me," the girl said as she rubbed her neck. "She said that I should have it because the stones were the same color as my lips."

"Are you all right now?" asked Gwendolyn.

"I think I should sit down," said the girl as she took a seat on a bench just outside the door. She didn't seem to notice the bear prince as he slipped away into the woods, but she smiled when Dog came over to be petted.

"Should we get someone for you?" asked Gwendolyn.

The girl shook her head. "No one's here except me. If you hadn't come along when you did...Oh, I forgot to thank you!" she said, blinking up at Annie. "That necklace was meant to kill me, I just know it!"

Liam frowned. "Why would anyone want to kill you?"

"Not just anyone; my stepmother. She must have found me somehow. My stepmother has always hated me, although I don't know why. She tried to have me killed when I was a little girl, but the huntsman who brought me into the forest let me go. I don't know if he was kind-hearted or if he just thought the wild animals would get me. I spent a night in the forest, then wandered around until I found this cottage. The dwarves who live here took me in and I've worked as their housekeeper ever since. My name is Snow White, by the way. The dwarves are always telling me not to talk to strangers, but I don't think you're strangers anymore, not after saving my life."

"You aren't related to a girl named Rose Red, are you? She has a sister named Snow White," said Gwendolyn.

Snow White shook her head. "I'm an only child."

"It must have been a popular name to give baby girls back then," Gwendolyn said, shrugging.

"I suppose," said Snow White. "But I thought my

name was unique. My nursemaid told me that my mother wanted a daughter with hair as black as coal and skin as white as snow. I was always grateful that I wasn't named Coal." Snow White gave them a little half smile, which faded away when she added, "My mother died when I was born. My father married my step-mother a few years later." Seeing their sympathetic expressions, she quickly said, "Well, enough about me. Tell me, why are you here?"

"We're looking for someone," said Liam. "A dwarf, actually. One who has lived somewhere else and would have just come home because of a family emergency."

"Seven dwarves live here," said Snow White. "They just fetched their brother home. Their grandfather is ailing and wanted to see them all together before he died. That's where they are now. I have no idea when they'll be back. It could be tonight, it could be next week."

Annie sat down beside her. "My name is Annie and this is my sister, Gwendolyn, and my friend Liam. We've come a long way to talk to the dwarf who just came home. Do you mind if we wait until they get back?"

"I wish you would," said Snow White, her eyes brightening as they met Annie's. "I'd enjoy your company. It isn't often that I have someone to talk to during the day, and I haven't talked to a girl close to my age in years. You and your sister can sleep in my room with me. It used to be the dwarves' parents' room. Your friend can sleep upstairs until the dwarves get home." She glanced shyly at Liam. "There are plenty of beds up there to choose from."

"Thank you," said Annie. "We'll be happy to help you in any way that we can while we're here."

"Oh, you don't have to do that," said Snow White. "Just having someone to talk to will be enough."

⁀

Although Gwendolyn said she was too tired to help, Annie insisted on working alongside Snow White. Annie scrubbed the kitchen table while Snow White used long paddles to take bread out of the brick oven and Gwendolyn grudgingly arranged flowers in a vase for the table. While Snow White started a pot of stew for supper, Annie swept the floor and Gwendolyn folded napkins, grumbling. Snow White whistled while she worked, which Annie found annoying, so she ignored both girls and studied the house while she cleaned.

The first floor of the cottage was one large room with a staircase in the middle dividing it in half. On one side of the staircase stood the kitchen, most of which was filled with a long table and the benches that sat on either side. A brick oven was set into the wall next to the large fireplace, which was also used for cooking. Opposite the fireplace stood a dry sink and a cupboard stacked high with eight sets of dishes, a basket filled with apples, another with onions, and a third stuffed with potatoes.

Large windows on either side of the room filled it with light, making it easy to see the carving that decorated every wooden surface. The legs of the table had been carved to look like tree trunks, the benches were covered with carved leaves and flowers, as were the cupboard and dry sink. The door and window frames, the beams on the ceiling, and the mantel above the fireplace had been decorated with the birds and animals of the forest, including unicorns, griffins, and dragons.

As Annie finished the kitchen floor and worked her way around to the other side of the staircase, she saw that this room had been decorated in a similar manner. Along with birds, animals, and plants, however, the artist had also included insects. Butterflies swarmed across the front of the fireplace, and dragonflies decorated the mantel, where flower candleholders rested. The carved faces of mice, chipmunks, and squirrels peeped between the vines growing over the backs of the eight chairs facing the fireplace. Although the carving had obviously been done by the same person, each chair was different from the others. Some had wide seats and thick cushions, some had thin cushions and deep seats, and one had a curved seat and no cushion at all.

"I can't wait for Liam to see this," Annie said when

Gwendolyn and Snow White walked into the room. "He loves to whittle." Liam had gone hunting with Dog and had yet to come inside the cottage.

"I'm going to make up the dwarves' beds," Snow White announced. "I washed the sheets this morning and they should be dry by now."

"I think I'll sit this one out," said Gwendolyn as she headed for the chair with the plumpest cushions.

The first thing Annie saw when they stepped through the back door was the garden. Butterflies danced over rows of carrots, onions, peas, beans, and cabbage. Rooster stalked through the rows, gobbling insects, while Cat slept in a patch of sunlight, his head pillowed on his paws.

Snow White led the way to a rope stretched from one tree to another just past the end of the garden. Eighteen short white sheets hung from the rope. "Cragery's sheets haven't been washed since he was here last," she said. "When I decided to wash his, I thought I might as well wash everyone's. Then I won't have to do them again until next week."

"Is Cragery the one who just came home?" asked Annie.

Snow White nodded. "He left home about nine years ago, before I arrived. Here, you can help me fold this." She handed the end of a sheet to Annie.

"Were the dwarves this good at keeping their own

house when you met them?" Annie asked as she set the sheet in the basket.

"Oh, no! The house was a terrible mess. That's why they let me stay. They said that there was no way I could do a worse job, even though I was young. I wasn't very good then, but I muddled through and got better over the years."

"Do you like living here?" asked Annie.

"Most of the time," said Snow White. "Although I do get lonely. You know, I've felt safe here for years, but now that my stepmother has found me, I don't know what I'm going to do."

"Are you sure it's her?"

"It has to be. I can't imagine that two women mean to kill me!"

"Didn't you recognize her when you saw her?"

Snow White shook her head. "But then I wouldn't necessarily. My stepmother is a witch and can make herself look however she wants. I tried to tell my father that, but he wouldn't listen. He wouldn't listen to anything I said once she came to live with us. Here we go—all done. Come on. I'll show you the upstairs."

Snow White divided the sheets in half so they could each carry some. They passed Gwendolyn, napping in one of the chairs, and started up the steps. Annie was delighted when they reached the top and saw the room where the dwarves slept. It was a bright, cheery room with a window in each wall. A trunk sat beside each of the eight beds, providing storage for personal possessions.

At first Annie thought that all the beds were identical, but as she helped Snow White make them up, she saw that each one was distinctive. She laughed when she saw the ducklings on the headboard of one bed and snarling lions on the bed beside it.

Snow White turned to see what Annie was looking at, and smiled. "Their father did all the carving. He built this house before Hummfree was born. Hummfree is the oldest. That's his bed over there," she said pointing across the room to a bed with an owl on the headboard. "The boys got to choose what he carved on their beds, but they were young and weren't always happy with their choices later."

"Who has the ducky bed?" asked Annie.

"That's Sheckley's. He can't stand it now. And the one with the lions is Shandy's. He's the youngest and was always the noisiest, so I think the roaring lion is still appropriate. I have to confess, I have secret names for each of them and his is Loud."

"Really? What are the others?"

"Promise you won't tell them, because I've never told anyone before and they'd be so hurt if they knew." Snow White waited until Annie nodded, then said, "Well, Hummfree thinks he knows everything and always has to be in charge, so I call him Bossy. Bilyum, who has the bluejays on his bed over there, speaks without thinking, and hurts people's feelings, so he's Rudie. I told you about Sheckley and his duck bed. He has bad allergies, so I call him Itchy. Bobbert has the bed over there. He can't sit still for a minute, so I call him Twitchy. The one with the cats with the creepy smiles? That's Dewane's bed. He reminds me of a tinker who would sell you a used pot with a leaky bottom while acting as if he's doing you a big favor. I call him Dodgy. Rigg sleeps over there in the bed with the fruit tarts pictured on the headboard. He's always hungry, and I guess he was when he was young, too. That's what I call him—Hungry. He loves my cooking more than anyone else, although I think he'd probably love any-one's cooking as long as he got to eat it."

"And what about that bed?" Annie asked, pointing to the far corner.

"That's Cragery's bed," said Snow White. "You prob-ably can't see it from here, but he has bags of gold on the headboard. He isn't a close friend of yours, is he?"

"I've never even met him," said Annie. She was reluctant to say much about the dwarf, or why they were there, because she didn't want to offend Snow White or make her angry enough to send them away.

"Good," said Snow White. "I don't want to insult a friend of yours, but from what I've heard about him, he isn't very nice. His brothers have told me that he's greedy and selfish, so I named him Greedy. I've been hoping that Cragery isn't that bad and that his brothers were exaggerating when they told stories about him, but from the little bit I saw of him, I think it was probably all true."

"I'm afraid I haven't heard anything good about him either," Annie told her.

"Ah," said Snow White. "Then you and your friends didn't come for a friendly visit."

Annie shrugged. "He may not be happy to see a certain friend of mine."

"I take it you don't mean your sister or your friend Liam," said Snow White. "So you must mean that bear I saw sneaking off into the woods."

"You saw him?" Annie asked, surprised. "You didn't mention it."

"Do you think I'd miss a bear so close to my house? Of course I saw him, but I figured he was enchanted, since I saw him talking to Gwendolyn. He is, isn't he? Enchanted, I mean."

"We think it was Cragery who enchanted him," said Annie.

"Really? I didn't know Cragery was *that* awful! Or that he could even do magic," Snow White said, looking thoughtful. "I hope he doesn't enchant one of his brothers. None of them like Cragery and they've been fighting with him ever since he showed up. He and Hummfree fought so much on the way home that they split up and came back separately. I love the dwarves as if they were my own brothers and I don't want to see anything bad happen to them. Although, if your bear friend doesn't like Cragery ... You know, I wasn't looking forward to seeing that nasty dwarf again, but now I can't wait to see what happens when he gets back to find a bear waiting for him!"

Chapter 19

THE THREE GIRLS TALKED LONG into the night, exchanging stories about what it was like to keep house for seven dwarves and what it was like to live at court. The only thing Snow White didn't want to talk about was her life before she came to stay with the dwarves, other than to say that her father had changed after he remarried. Even so, by the time they stopped talking, Annie felt so comfortable with Snow White that it seemed as if they had known each other for years.

Later, as Snow White and Gwendolyn fell asleep, Annie lay on a pallet on the floor beside her sister, thinking about Snow White. Although she acted like an ordinary girl, Snow White wasn't ordinary at all. She was as beautiful as a princess, and when Annie had touched her to remove the necklace, the girl's beauty had faded. Annie hadn't seen Beldegard since they arrived at the cottage, and hadn't had a chance to talk to Liam alone after he returned from hunting, so she resolved to talk to both of them as soon as she could and ask if any royal princesses were missing.

The next morning, Annie and Gwendolyn joined Snow White in the garden as she weeded between the vegetable rows. The three girls knelt side by side, tossing the weeds in an old basket. Gwendolyn was less diligent than the other two, missing half the weeds and not pulling out all the roots, but Annie was pleased that her sister was trying.

They worked in silence for a time, enjoying the songs of the birds in the nearby trees and the warmth of the sun on their faces as Quentin foraged and Rooster scratched the dirt at the end of the rows. Cat was already taking a nap, stretched out in the sunlight, while Dog was off exploring the trees near the cottage.

They had worked for nearly an hour, moving along the rows, when Annie sat up and stretched, trying to ease a cramp in her back. She was about to say something to her companions when she heard whimpering and something running through the forest.

"What's that?" she asked, getting to her feet. Suddenly Dog came floundering out of the trees, slobbering and looking wild-eyed.

Annie raced toward Dog who was pawing at her mouth and whining. Something red flashed below her jaw and her whine grew louder. "It's the necklace!" Annie cried even as she dropped to her knees beside

Dog. The ruby necklace was wrapped around the dog's lower jaw, squeezing so hard that it was smaller than a bracelet. Annie's hand shot out and grabbed the necklace, which relaxed and stretched back to its normal size. Pulling the necklace from the dog's mouth, she held it up to examine it. "Apparently this is too dangerous to leave lying around," said Annie.

Stuffing the necklace into her pocket to deal with later, Annie examined Dog's mouth, then ruffled her fur while the animal panted and tried to lick her. "Calm down!" Annie said, laughing. "You're all right now!" She was too close for Dog to be able to talk, so she patted her one last time and looked around until she found a stick of just the right size. "If you want to play," said Annie, "you should stay with sticks." When Annie hurled the stick, Dog ran after it, barking, her tail wagging furiously.

◦

The three girls worked together until the sun was high overhead. Annie let her mind wander, and though she had asked Snow White many questions the night before, she thought of one more. "Why did Cragery leave home when he did?" she asked as she tossed another weed in the basket.

"As I understand it," said Snow White, "he worked in the family's mine with his brothers for a time before deciding that he hated it, so he left home to get a job at the castle. He became the court jester, but he wasn't very funny and people were mean to him. Finally he broke down, ranting that he was tired of all the short jokes, and left still wearing his pointy cap and jingly bells. It seems he took a valuable piece of the queen's jewelry with him, but no one knew where he went, so they couldn't track him down. His brothers didn't hear from him for a long time, then a few years ago Hummfree received a letter. Hummfree never said—"

"Yoo-hoo! Anyone home?" called a voice from around the corner of the cottage. A horse nickered and Quentin raised his head, still chewing the leaf that stuck out of his mouth.

"Are the dwarves back?" asked Gwendolyn.

Snow White shook her head. "That was a woman's voice. I'd better go see what she wants."

"We'll go with you," said Annie, brushing off her knees as she stood.

Gwendolyn wiped her hair out of her eyes as she got to her feet, leaving a smudge of dirt on her no longer flawless forehead. She had been sitting so close to Annie that her beauty had faded, leaving her pretty rather than gorgeous.

Liam had gone hunting again, so the girls were the only ones there. Dog joined them as they hurried to the front of the cottage, where a young woman sitting on the bench seat of a tinker's wagon waited with the reins in her hands, watching the door.

"May I help you?" Snow White said while Annie studied the stranger with growing concern. She had seen tinkers come to her parents' castle, but none of them had looked like this. It was true that the woman was dressed in the rough gown and cap of a tinker's wife, but her wagon looked fairly new and her horse wasn't tired and worn like most tinkers' horses. In fact, the horse was a lovely bay with bright eyes and a long, well-groomed tail and mane, more like a noble's horse than a tinker's.

The woman turned at the sound of Snow White's voice and seemed surprised to see her. "It's you! I mean...Hello! I've brought prime goods to show you. Pots and pans and some, uh..." The woman glanced at Annie and Gwendolyn, then turned away as if they were beneath her notice. "Say, is there anyone else here? Another young lady, perhaps a particularly beautiful one?"

"It's just us," Annie was quick to say. She could hear the same high-pitched hum that she'd heard when the old woman had been there the day before. There was magic present and it wasn't the good kind.

"Are you sure?" said the woman, leaning forward to peer through the closest window.

"I'm sure," said Annie. "And we don't want to buy anything, so you needn't wait."

The woman glanced at Annie again, then back to where Gwendolyn was standing. Because she and Annie were no longer near each other, her beauty had begun to return. Annie saw the way the woman was looking at her sister, and hurried to stand between them.

"We're quite sure," said Annie. "You don't have anything we need."

Dog must have picked up on the tone of her voice, because she pinned back her ears and began to growl at the woman.

"But I have good sturdy pots and pans. I even have lovely combs for beautiful girls," she said, glancing from Annie to where Dog stood with her hackles raised.

"Good day," Annie said, and turned to herd Gwendolyn, Snow White, and Dog into the cottage. After closing and locking the door behind them, Annie peered out the window at the woman, who looked angry as she jerked at the reins and left.

When the woman was gone, Annie crouched down beside Dog. "I have a task for you. I want you and Cat to follow the woman. Stay as close to her as you can and see where she goes and what she does." Glancing up at Snow White, she added, "That's the same woman who gave you that necklace yesterday, I'm sure of it."

"Oh, I don't doubt it," said Snow White. "Hardly anyone ever comes this way. Two strangers trying to sell me something within days of each other is too unusual to be a coincidence."

❦

Annie and Snow White were clearing the table after supper that night when they heard a soft tapping at the door. "I'll get it," Liam said as he set down the knife he'd been sharpening. When he opened the door a crack, Cat poked his head in, looked around, and sauntered over to Gwendolyn, who was sitting at the table embroidering napkins.

"I'm starving," said Cat, rubbing against her legs. "Did you save me some supper?"

"Another enchanted animal?" Snow White asked in surprise. "Are all the animals you brought with you enchanted?"

"Not like the bear," Annie told her. "Cat and the others were never human."

"You told her about Beldegard?" said Liam.

Annie glanced at him and shrugged. "She guessed."

"About that food—" said Cat.

"Not until you tell me what you learned," Annie told him.

Cat sighed and leaped up into Gwendolyn's lap, where he shoved his head into her hand until she began to pet him. "Dog and I followed the woman to a castle, where they let her in without any questions," said Cat. "From the way they jumped when she told them what to do, I'd say they were afraid of her. Anyway, she left the horse and cart in the courtyard and went up a lot of steps to a big, drafty tower room. Dog couldn't get past the guard downstairs, but I followed her all the way to the top and slipped through the door behind her. I had a quick look around while she fiddled with the door lock. She had bottles full of little dead stuff, and a stack of old, dusty books that smelled bad, just like our master used to keep locked in his secret room. That woman is a witch, if you ask me."

"Just tell us what you saw," said Liam.

"I was still watching her when she stepped in front of a big, tall mirror. The frame was shiny gold, but the glass was dark and murky. 'Mirror, mirror, on the wall,' she said. 'Who's the fairest one of all?'"

Snow White looked outraged. "That's why she wanted to kill me? Because she thinks I'm pretty?"

"Why was she talking to a mirror?" asked Gwendolyn.

"It wasn't a regular mirror," said Cat. "As soon as she asked it a question, a frightening face appeared, kind of floating in the glass. It was a woman's face; she reminded me of the neighbor who used to yell when I sang outside her window at night."

"And what did the face in the mirror do?" Annie asked.

"She looked annoyed and said, 'What's wrong? You got wax in your ears? I told you yesterday that Princess Gwendolyn, the most beautiful princess in all the kingdoms, has arrived in Helmswood.'"

Gwendolyn gasped and her hand stilled. "So now she's after me?"

"Do you want me to finish telling you or not?" Cat asked.

"Sorry," said Gwendolyn, and she resumed petting the cat.

"'And where might I find this princess?' the woman asked the mirror in a voice as sweet as honey.

"'At the dwarves' cottage, as I already told you,' said the face in the mirror. 'What's the matter with you? Don't you hear anything I say?'

"That's when the witch's face got red. She pointed a finger at the mirror and shouted, 'I'd watch what I say if I were you! If you're not careful, you'll end up back in that dark little closet where I found you. I imagine the spiders and roaches will be happy to see you again. Or maybe I'll drop you in the moat for a day or two. I hear it's swarming with water snakes.'"

"So she's threatening the face in her magic mirror?" said Annie.

"That's what it sounded like," said Cat. "But the face just laughed and said, 'You think that would matter to me? At least then I wouldn't have to answer the same questions over and over and could have some peace and quiet!'

"'I'm warning you . . . ,' said the woman.

"'Fine, be that way,' the face told her. 'Princess Gwendolyn is still at the dwarves' cottage along with her sister, Annabelle.' And then the face in the mirror moved over and Gwendolyn's and Annie's faces floated up like bubbles in a pond. It was kind of scary and I could feel the fur rising on my—"

"Cat! Just tell us what happened next!" said Liam.

"All right, all right! So, the woman said, 'But I saw those girls! That Annabelle looks the same, but the other one isn't nearly as beautiful as you say.'

"'Probably because of Annabelle,' said the face in the mirror. 'She has the ability to—'

"'I knew it!' said the woman. 'She's a witch, too! I thought there was something different about her.'

"'I never said—' the face began, but the woman didn't want to hear anything more it had to say.

"'I'll go back tomorrow morning wearing my best disguise,' said the woman. 'That girl won't be able to hide her sister from me a second time.'

"The face tried again, saying, 'But she isn't—'

"'Quiet! I know what I have to do!' the woman shouted.

"'Fine!' said the face in the mirror. 'If you don't want to hear what I have to say, you can do whatever you want!'

"The woman walked away then and started making some stinky brew in an old metal pot. I left through the window as soon as I could and skedaddled back here."

"You did an excellent job, Cat!" Annie told him. Gwendolyn began to scratch behind his ears and Annie could hear his purr all the way across the room.

"Where's Dog?" asked Liam.

"She stayed behind to keep an eye on the woman," Cat replied. "Dog was able to mingle with the other dogs in the castle and can go just about anywhere. I'm sure she'll be back as soon as she has something important to tell you. A little to the left," Cat said, turning his body and arching his neck into Gwendolyn's hand.

Chapter 20

Annie, Gwendolyn, and Snow White were watching through the window for the woman when she showed up the next morning. For once, Liam hadn't gone hunting; he joined them at the door when they heard an old woman's wavery voice.

"Apples, fresh apples!" she cried from the walk leading up to the door.

"Doesn't she realize that we usually don't have visitors more than two or three times a year?" Snow White whispered to Annie. "I'd have to be a numskull not to be suspicious of a third visit in a row, even if she did change the way she looks. And she wants us to believe that she came all this way to sell a couple of apples?"

"I don't think she thinks about things like that," Annie whispered back.

"Have you had your breakfast yet?" the old woman called. "I have some nice fresh apples for sale!"

When Liam reached for the door, Annie shook her head. "I'll handle this. She has magic, remember?" She opened the door and stepped outside, but before she could close it her friends piled out after her.

This time the witch looked like a stooped old woman with a heavily wrinkled face. Her washed-out blue eyes opened wide in surprise when she saw them, but she recovered quickly and said, "Oh, my, there's so many of you! Well, that's all right. I have plenty. And an extra nice one for you, beautiful girl."

Gwendolyn had been standing close enough to Annie that her beauty had faded a little, but not as much as the day before. When the witch offered her the most perfect-looking apple in her basket, she took a step back.

Annie plucked the apple from the witch's hand. The old woman scowled at her as Annie examined the apple with distaste. "That's not for you!" the witch shrilled. "Give it to your sister!"

"How do you know she's my sister?" Annie asked her.

The old woman spluttered as she glanced from one girl to the other. When Gwendolyn was beautiful, she and Annie didn't look enough alike to make anyone think they were related. "I just…I thought…"

"Don't worry, *old woman*," said Annie. "You don't need to bother coming up with a plausible lie. We know why you're here and that this apple is poisoned." Pulling her arm back, Annie hurled the apple at a tree so that the fruit smashed against the trunk. Turning back to the witch, she added, "Now leave and don't come back, no matter what you make yourself look like!"

The witch glowered at Annie. "How dare you talk to me that way! Do you know what I could do to you?"

"Nothing!" growled a deep voice. "You leave them alone or I'll do something *you* won't like."

Suddenly Beldegard was back, looking more ferocious than Annie had ever seen him. He stood at the edge of the forest, his lips curled in a snarl. When the witch glanced his way but didn't move, he started toward her at a shambling run. He'd gone only a few steps when the witch flung aside her basket of apples and dashed into the woods. The bear prince ran after her, crashing through the underbrush.

"He didn't need to do that," said Annie. "I could have handled the woman."

కా

Beldegard had yet to return when the dwarves arrived. The moment Snow White heard them, she ran out of the cottage and flung her arms around the oldest, then went from dwarf to dwarf, hugging each one in turn. Annie had followed her out of the cottage and was pleased to see that the seven dwarves seemed equally happy to see Snow White. They looked like nice people and even though Snow White was much taller than any of them and not related by blood, they behaved as if they were family.

It was easy to tell that the dwarves were related to one another, however. They all had the same-shape nose—straight with a little bump on the end, and the same strong chin, but some of them were handsome and some were not, some had long hair and some had short. The only dwarf with a beard was Cragery, the eighth dwarf, whom Snow White did not even try to hug.

The dwarf's long, white beard hung almost to his feet. Both his beard and the mustache that curled around his lips were stained and spotted with food. Unlike his seven brothers, who looked at Annie with twinkling, friendly eyes, Cragery's gaze was cold and hostile. He didn't even seem to notice Snow White as he continued arguing with his brothers.

"I can't believe you dragged me all the way home for that!" groused Cragery in a half-strangled voice.

"Grandfather said he was dying and wanted to see us all together one last time. Aren't you glad he recovered?" said the dwarf with the stooped back and wrinkled face, who Annie thought must be Hummfree, the oldest of the brothers.

Cragery shrugged. "I don't care one way or the other. He's not leaving me anything in his will. He told me so yesterday! That old dwarf has hated me since the first day he saw me."

The dwarf scratching a rash on his neck scowled when he said, "You punched him in the nose and broke it!"

"I was a baby!" said Cragery. "That's what babies do!"

A dwarf with slicked-down hair snorted, while another brother said, "Not usually!"

Cragery sneered at his brothers. "I've always been special, and you know it!"

"Is that what you call it?" asked Hummfree. "Were you being *special* when you ran off to work at the castle when we needed your help in the mines? Were you being *special* when you stole that trinket from the queen and disappeared for years? And what about when I went to fetch you home and you were rude and nasty to everyone we met? Were you being *special* then, too?"

"It wasn't just a trinket that he stole from the queen," said Beldegard from the edge of the forest. Everyone turned; more than one dwarf reached for the ax on his belt as the bear prince emerged from the trees. "The witch had given it magical properties that he learned about when he worked in the castle."

"Stand back!" shouted an imperious voice as Prince Maitland and his men trotted down the road toward the cottage. "That's the dangerous beast I've been hunting.

Go into your home now so that I might kill it and no one else will get hurt."

"No!" Gwendolyn cried as she ran from the cottage door to throw her arms around Beldegard. "He is not dangerous and he's not a beast. He's my beloved Beldegard and your own brother, who was enchanted by that evil dwarf."

Snow White nudged Annie and leaned toward her to whisper, "I knew it would be interesting when the dwarves came home, but I never imagined it would be like this! Who is that incredibly handsome man?" she asked, gazing at Prince Maitland, her eyes filled with longing.

"That's Beldegard's brother. Beldegard is the bear prince."

"The bear is a prince? Then that means his brother is one, too! Tell me, is anyone else coming?"

"I don't think so," Annie whispered back. "Unless... Yes, there he is. Yardley is here as well. It looks as if Maitland captured him."

Snow White peered past the mounted prince to where a wolf was cowering at the end of a long, knotted rope. "Is the wolf enchanted?"

Annie nodded. "Just like Beldegard."

"This is so exciting!" Snow White breathed.

While they were talking, Maitland dismounted and approached Gwendolyn and Beldegard on foot with his sword drawn. "Stand aside, beautiful lady," Maitland said. "That beast has lied to you. My brother is dead."

"No, he's not!" Annie called as she hurried to her sister's side, but Liam was already there with his sword unsheathed, facing Maitland.

"He is our friend and a true prince," Liam announced in a loud voice so everyone could hear. "Anyone who harms him will answer to me."

"Please, kind sir," Snow White cried, hurrying to Maitland's side. "These people are my friends and would not lie!"

When Maitland glanced down at her, his gaze softened and he lowered his arm.

Annie turned toward where she had last seen Cragery, but he was no longer there. "Stop him!" she cried when she spotted him sneaking into the forest. "Gwendolyn told the truth! That dwarf changed Beldegard into a bear. We've traveled a long way to make him turn the bear prince back into a man!"

The dwarves turned toward Cragery, but not one of them made a move to go after him when he began to run. It was Liam who followed the dwarf and grabbed him by the back of his tunic. Hefting Cragery onto his shoulder, Liam carried the kicking, swearing dwarf back to the clearing.

Bright splotches of pink stained Snow White's cheeks when she turned to the seven dwarves saying, "He's been a horrible person and you're just going to let him get away with it? Don't you understand how much he's hurt people?"

"Are these accusations true, Brother?" Hummfree asked. "Have you harmed others with a magic object?"

"No, of course not!" said Cragery. "I don't have to stand here and listen to such blatant lies! Let me go. I knew I shouldn't come back here!"

"It is true!" shouted Yardley. The wolf had come as close as he could on the end of the rope and was straining to get closer. "He turned me into a wolf for no reason at all!"

"You were cheating at cards," said Cragery, his face turning red when he realized what he'd said.

"Then it is true!" said Hummfree. "It's one thing when you are unkind to your family. We put up with it for years because you are our brother. But we cannot condone mistreating others! We will see that he is punished for what he has done," he said, turning to Liam and Beldegard.

"There's more to it than that," said Annie. "He has to turn Beldegard and Yardley back into humans. There are others as well—three brothers he turned into pigs and a family that now lives as bears. And those are only the ones we've happened to meet."

Hummfree nodded. "Show me this magical object, Cragery," he ordered his brother.

Cragery shrugged the other dwarves' hands off his

arms and reached into his pocket. He pulled out a large brooch made of intricately wrought gold surrounding a dragon's head made of sapphires. When Hummfree reached for it, Cragery held it close to his chest, saying, "It's mine! No one can touch it but me."

"No one wants the stupid thing," Annie told him. "Just use it to turn everyone back!"

"What will I get if I do?" Cragery asked, rubbing his thumb over the dragon's face.

Liam took a step closer, his hand on the hilt of his sword. "You'll get to stay alive."

"You can't do anything to me!" shouted Cragery, raising the brooch to eye level. "Not if I turn you into a woodchuck!"

A flash of blue light shot from the brooch, slamming Liam in the chest. The light knocked him back so that he staggered as the blue light spread up his neck and across his face, down his torso to his legs and feet. He stood there for a moment, looking stunned. Suddenly there was a loud *pop!* and Liam disappeared, leaving behind a plump, bright-eyed woodchuck.

Annie jerked as if she had been hit as well. "No!" she screamed. "You can't do that! Not to Liam!"

"Annie?" said the woodchuck. "What just happened?" He looked confused, as did everyone else in the clearing. The seven dwarves stared at Cragery as if he had two heads.

Annie rushed toward the dwarf, ready to throttle

him if necessary, shouting, "You turn him back, right this instant!"

"Get away from me!" he yelled, holding up the brooch again.

The light hit Annie with a crackling sound, bounced off and slammed into Cragery, knocking him to the ground. He lay there, whimpering as the light spread, covering him until he was completely blue. There was a loud *pop* and the dwarf was gone. A gray squirrel lay on its back, its legs scrabbling in the air. Three more *pop*s followed a moment later. The wolf, the bear, and the woodchuck were gone. Instead, a handsome young man crouched beside Gwendolyn and another, more ordinary man, squatted on all fours with a rope around his neck. Liam stood, still holding his sword, looking bemused.

While Hummfree grabbed the squirrel, Annie threw herself into Liam's arms. Liam dropped the sword in time to catch her and swing her off her feet. Her first kiss landed on his nose, but the rest landed on his lips. If he wouldn't kiss her, there wasn't any reason that she couldn't kiss him. Except...She pulled back for a moment, wondering if he might not *want* her to kiss him. After all...And then he was dragging her closer to kiss her again. Annie lost track of time as Liam kissed her most thoroughly.

"I don't know what I would have done if I'd lost you," she murmured when she could speak again. She reached up to brush aside a lock of hair that had fallen over his eyes, and smiled when he turned his head to kiss her hand. "I wouldn't have jumped on you like that, but when you turned back into a human, I just had to kiss you. To be honest, I've been waiting for you to kiss me."

"I've never thought people should show their affection in public, but I've changed my mind. I don't care who sees me kiss you now. I've missed out on too many kissing opportunities with you already."

"Annie, Liam, I'd like you to meet my intended, Prince Beldegard," Gwendolyn interrupted. When they turned around, she was holding the prince's hand and gazing at him with such love that tears prickled the backs of Annie's eyelids.

Annie'd had a fairly good idea of what Beldegard looked like when he wasn't a bear, but he'd never looked completely human the way he did now. He was a big man, standing well over six feet tall. His hair was the same rich brown shade that his fur had been when he was a bear. Annie found his brown eyes flecked with gold appealing and liked the way his mouth quirked to one side when he smiled.

"I must admit, you made a great bear, but an even better prince," Annie told him.

"Maybe now we can go home?" Gwendolyn said, sounding hopeful. "We want to get married as soon as possible."

Annie glanced at Snow White, who had followed the

dwarves to the door of the cottage. None of the dwarves seemed upset that their brother had just been turned into a squirrel. "We'll go soon, but not quite yet," Annie told her sister. "There's something we have to take care of before we leave."

"Ahem," said Maitland at Beldegard's shoulder. "I'm glad to see you're back. Mother and Father will be overjoyed."

"Are you sorry you're not going to be King of Montrose someday?" asked Beldegard.

"Not at all!" said Maitland, then gave a little laugh. "Well, maybe a bit. When everyone thought you were dead, I got used to the idea that I might actually be king. Then when we heard a rumor that you had been turned into a bear, my friends convinced me to make sure you didn't come back and take away my inheritance. Although it wasn't really my inheritance, was it?"

"No, it wasn't. And if it really was your friends' idea, you might want to get new friends," Beldegard told Maitland, eyeing the men who had stayed by the horses.

Maitland laughed again. "I think you're right."

"But you might not have to give up your aspirations for being a king," said Beldegard. "That lovely young lady who seems so enamored of you is Snow White, the daughter of the king of Helmswood."

"Really?" said Maitland, turning toward the doorway where Snow White was still talking to the dwarves.

Annie glanced at Beldegard, who shrugged and said, "We're in Helmswood, so that's the closest castle. The witch was the queen of Helmswood and Snow White's stepmother."

Annie nodded. "You're right. And she told us that she's an only child."

"Really?" said Maitland.

"So whoever marries her—"

"Yes, yes, I got that part. I do think she's lovely. All that long, black hair..."

"Just be forewarned," said Annie. "Snow White has lots of people who care about her and would be angry if you broke her heart."

"And an angry witch stepmother!" added Liam.

"I'll keep that in mind," Maitland said as he started toward Snow White.

"As for you," Beldegard said, turning to Gwendolyn, "we have a lot to talk about."

"Really?" she said, smiling up at him.

"Really!" said Beldegard, and he led her around the corner to the back of the cottage.

"We have a lot to talk about, too," Liam told Annie. "But first I'd like to get cleaned up. Beldegard may be used to smelling like a bear, but I don't like smelling like a woodchuck."

Annie laughed and tilted her head to gaze into his eyes. "I don't mind."

"But I do," Liam told her. "When we have the conversation that I want to have, I want everything to be perfect."

Annie was watching him go toward the well when she heard the sound of horses' hooves on packed dirt. She glanced back to see that Maitland's men were leading the horses to a shed on the other side of the cottage. Only Yardley was left, gingerly touching his neck where the rope had scraped him. When he looked up and saw Annie, he smiled, waved good-bye, and sauntered toward the road, whistling a merry tune.

She was about to go inside when she noticed something sparkling in the grass. Taking a step closer, she realized that it was the dragon-head brooch. Although Annie wasn't sure what she should do with it, she picked it up and stuck it in her pocket with the necklace. At least when she had the brooch, it wasn't likely to hurt anyone.

"Annie!" called Dog from the woods on the other side of the road. "I have to tell you what happened!"

"Don't come any closer," Annie reminded Dog when he was a few yards away. "You won't be able to talk if you do."

Dog sat down, her tongue lolling to the side. "I was with the other dogs in the castle this morning when I saw the queen put something in the king's drink. The other dogs told me that she did it every morning. He talked like a person before he drank his drink, but

246

afterward he didn't talk much at all. She did all the talking then."

"She must be drugging him," said Annie. "Good job, Dog! Now we know what we have to do. I don't know where Cat is, but Rooster is still in the garden. I want the two of you to go to the castle. Be in the hall where the king and queen eat before breakfast tomorrow morning. Do whatever you have to do to make sure that the queen doesn't put anything in the king's drink. I'll be there as early as I can to deal with her."

CHAPTER 21

ANNIE WOULD HAVE BEEN HAPPY to go to the castle
with just Liam and Snow White, but Gwendolyn, Beldegard, and Maitland insisted on going with them.
Arriving at the castle in the half-light of early dawn,
they found the drawbridge already down and the courtyard bustling. Four guards met them at the gate. Three
guards were surly and demanded to know who they
were and why they were there, but the fourth guard
looked past the three princes to Snow White and his
face lit up in a huge smile. "Your Highness," he said. "It's
you!"

Snow White stepped to the front of the line. "I wasn't
sure anyone would recognize me. It's been so long."

"I wasn't likely to forget our little princess!" said the
guard. "Don't mind these fools, they've been here only
a few years, but I remember the old days when you
were always underfoot and folks in the castle were

lighthearted. Those were dark days indeed when we thought you had wandered off in the woods and a wild animal had . . . Well, that's neither here nor there, now that you're back! Your father will be overjoyed to see you. I'd be honored to take you to him myself."

"I'd like that," Snow White said. "My friends will be coming with me." She looked pleased when Maitland took her arm, then glanced back as the rest of her companions hurried to enter the castle behind them.

It was a large castle, although not as impressive as some. The corridors were not as clean as the castle in Treecrest, nor as lavishly furnished as the castle in Floradale. When they entered the great hall, the rushes on the floor were in need of changing, and the wall-hangings were dingy with accumulated grime.

Annie wasn't surprised that Dog had blended in so well with the other dogs of the castle. She counted fourteen, and saw more snuffling through the rushes under the tables and asleep in inconvenient places where people had to step over them. Annie looked for the king in the great hall, but the guard led them through one door and out the other side, then down a broad corridor to a more private chamber. Even before the guard opened the door, Annie knew that there were dogs there as well from the racket they were making inside the room.

The guard frowned as he flung the door open and rushed inside as if he expected trouble. At first there was so much confusion that Annie couldn't tell what was going on. Snow White shouted, "Father!" and ran toward the man trying to chase Rooster away from the tall, dark-haired woman near the table at the far end. Dog was one of five hounds barking at the woman, although they could just as well have been barking at the bird that was flying at her face and trying to peck her hands.

"Dog, Rooster, that's enough!" Annie called as she hurried toward them.

Rooster flew to a rafter, out of reach of the humans below. After a few less-frenzied barks, the dogs quieted down as well.

The king had turned at the sound of Snow White's voice. Seeing her running toward him, his haggard eyes lit up and he sent a bench crashing to the floor in his rush to meet her. "My little girl," he murmured as he enfolded her in his arms.

"Distract the queen while Snow White and I talk to her father," Annie whispered to Liam, who had followed her across the room.

Snow White and the king were still talking in quiet voices when Annie herded them to the far corner, away from where the queen was already talking to Liam. "I have so much to tell you, Father," Snow White told him. "And none of it is good. It's about Marissa, your queen."

At the mention of the queen's name, Snow White's

father frowned. "What about her? I know you never got along with her."

Snow White sighed. "It's much more than just not getting along. She's a witch, Father. I tried to tell you years ago, but you wouldn't listen. She was probably drugging you even then."

"Drugging me? What are you talking about?" said the king.

"The queen has been slipping something into your drink every morning," said Annie. "We have witnesses who can tell you what they saw."

"I didn't get lost in the woods, Father, or at least not intentionally," Snow White said. "The queen had the huntsman take me there to kill me, but he let me go and I ran off. Some good people took me in, but the queen found me and tried to kill me again."

Annie nodded. "She brought Snow White a necklace to choke the life out of her."

"Who are you?" asked the king. "How do you know all this?"

"I'm Princess Annabelle of Treecrest. I was on a quest with my sister and our friends when I met Snow White. I was able to take the necklace from around her throat."

"If she hadn't, I would have died!" cried Snow White.

The king frowned and glanced at his wife, then back to the two girls. "I need proof if I'm to act on this."

"I have proof," said Annie as she reached into her pocket.

"Be careful, Father," Snow White said when he took the necklace from Annie.

The king turned the necklace over to examine it. "I gave her this the day we were wed!"

"She must have used her magic on it," Annie told him. "Now it will choke whoever wears it. If the queen is innocent, she won't mind putting on the necklace."

"But if she did what we say she did, she won't want to put it on, knowing what it will do," said Snow White.

"That should be proof enough," her father said, sounding grim. "Leave this up to me."

Annie turned around and saw that Liam, Gwendolyn, Beldegard, and Maitland had surrounded the queen and were talking to her in loud voices. Whenever the queen tried to peer around any of them to see the king, they stepped in front of her again, blocking her view and preventing her from going to him.

The king strode toward the front of the room, calling, "Guard!"

The man who had escorted Snow White and her friends had been waiting by the door as if he wasn't sure what to do. When the king called out, the guard ran to his side. Annie couldn't hear what the king told him, but a moment later the guard hurried out of the room and down the corridor.

"What are you doing, Archibald?" the queen demanded in a querulous voice.

"Dealing with something I should have taken care of a long time ago," said the king.

Half a dozen guards came running into the room and lined up against the wall to await further orders.

Liam and the others stepped away from the queen as the king approached her. The queen shot Annie a look of hatred before turning back to the king. "Do you remember this necklace?" he asked her, holding it up so all could see. "I gave it to you on the day we were wed and you said you'd cherish it forever."

"My necklace!" said the queen. "It was stolen, my lord. I didn't know how to tell you, but I'm so glad you got it back."

"Here, my dear," he said, holding it out to her. "Take off the one you're wearing now and wear this one instead."

The queen's voice was shaky when she laughed. Annie noticed that her face had gone pale and she kept wetting her lips with the tip of her tongue. "There's no need," said the queen. "I'll wear it tomorrow."

"I want to see it on you today," said the king.

The queen shook her head. "I can't. Don't you see, it wouldn't go with my gown."

"Guards," said the king, gesturing to the men by the wall. "The queen is not to leave this room until she has put on this necklace."

"No!" cried the queen. "I don't know what that horrid girl told you, but she's lying! This is some kind of trick. She's done something to the necklace. Perhaps she's poisoned it. Yes, that has to be it. I won't put that necklace on unless she does first!"

"Are you accusing my daughter of something so loathsome as attempting to poison you?" the king roared.

"No, of course not," the queen said, taking a step back. "I meant the other girl. The plain one there beside Snow White. She's a witch, I'm sure of it! Look. She doesn't want to wear it."

The king was about to reply when Annie spoke up. "I'll try it on. The necklace isn't poisoned."

"That won't be necessary," the king began, but the queen snatched the necklace from his grasp and slipped it around Annie's neck before anyone moved to stop her.

"Now if I die, you'll die first, little interfering witch," she whispered in Annie's ear so no one else could hear her.

"Take it off!" said the king.

Annie shook her head and laid her hand across the necklace, holding it in place. "It isn't hurting me," she said, then moved her hand so he could see. After a minute had passed and nothing had happened, Annie took off the necklace and handed it back to the king. "Now let her try it," she said, glancing from the king to the queen.

Queen Marissa stared at her, openmouthed. When the king handed the necklace to her, she smiled a secret kind of smile, and slipped the necklace around her own neck. "There," she said. "I'm wearing it. I don't know what all the fuss was about. I'm going to my chamber now and if…" The queen got a strange look in her eyes and put her hand to her throat. "No!" she gasped, clutching at the necklace, which was growing tighter with each passing second. "But it didn't do this to you!"

"It couldn't," said Annie. "Magic doesn't work on me."

"I'm torn," said the king. "I could just let the necklace do what her magic intended it to do, or I could take it off and lock her in the dungeon. Drugging a king and trying to kill a princess are certainly enough cause to convict her of treason."

"Take the necklace off her, Father!" cried Snow White. "I can't bear to see anyone suffer like that!"

"I'll do it," offered Annie, and once again the necklace relaxed at her touch. "Whatever you do, don't let her go back to her chamber. She has a secret room where she does her magic. Look in the tower for a locked door. My source tells me that she has all sorts of magic paraphernalia there."

"You see, she is a witch! She does have magic!" the queen called as the guards led her away.

Annie shook her head. "I don't have any magic, but I do have lots of friends."

⁊ઐ

Everyone was delighted to have Snow White back and the wicked queen locked away. The king was so happy that he declared the day a holiday and ordered the preparation of the biggest feast they had ever held. He invited Annie and her friends to stay as long as they wanted, but they were eager to get on the road as soon as possible. Although he tried insisting that they stay, he gave in when Annie promised that she and Liam would come back for a visit as soon as they could.

It was Snow White who kept delaying their departure. First she insisted that they eat an enormous breakfast, then she wanted to thank them for all they had done to help her. Annie and her friends were still eating when Snow White left to look for presents to give them. A few minutes later, Dog and Rooster came to say good-bye to Annie.

"I'm going to stay with Snow White," said Dog, careful to keep her distance. "She's asked me to stay, and I've made a lot of friends already. They tell me that no one cares about a dog's age here and it seems like a good place to live out my years."

"If that's what you want," said Annie. "I'm so glad I got to know you! Thank you for all your help."

"No, thank you!" said Dog. "I don't know where I

would have ended up if it hadn't been for you and your friends."

Annie sighed and crouched down. "Come here, Dog. I'm going to miss you!" When the dog bounded toward her and licked her face, Annie nearly fell over. Dog was still licking her when she wrapped her arms around the animal and whispered into her fur, "I never had a dog of my own. If I ever do, I want her to be just like you!"

"It's my turn now," Rooster squawked. "No hugs. No kisses. The pigs offered us a home. I'm going there to live. Quentin's going too."

"That sounds like a good plan," said Annie.

"Cat already told me that he wants to stay with the dwarves," Gwendolyn told her as Annie got to her feet. "They're spoiling him and he said that they have enough mice to keep him busy for years. The animals aren't staying together, so he said that they don't need the tablecloth. They gave it to Beldegard and me as a wedding present."

"That's a very nice present!" said Annie. "But I thought Cat would go home with you. The two of you really seemed to hit it off."

Gwendolyn shrugged. "I thought so, too, but he said he doesn't like to travel. It's all right. I'm going to be busy with the wedding and won't have much time for anything else."

"There you are!" Snow White said, although they

were still sitting where she had left them. "I have your presents ready for you. They're waiting in the court-yard. Come on, I want to show them to you."

"I hope it's nothing bulky," Liam told Annie as they followed Snow White out the door. "Whatever it is, we'll have to lug it all the way home."

"I don't think that will be a problem," Annie told him as they stepped into the courtyard.

Four horses stood waiting for them, saddled and ready to go. Annie glanced at her companions and saw that both Liam and Beldegard were smiling. "Maybe the trip back won't take too long after all," said Belde-gard. "Let's check them out," he told Liam.

"Father is sending twenty knights with you also," Snow White told her as the two princes strode toward the horses. "He's truly grateful for all your help in bring-ing me home. He wanted to send you in our gilded carriage, but I told him that would take too long and you wanted to get home as soon as possible."

"This is wonderful!" Annie told her. "We couldn't have asked for more."

"It's nothing, compared to what you've done for me. I would have died if it hadn't been for you. I can't wait until you come back to visit."

"You'll have to come to Treecrest first," said Gwen-dolyn. "Beldegard and I are going to send you an invita-tion to our wedding as soon as we set the date."

The princess looked up when Maitland and his men

rode from the stable into the courtyard. The young prince looked distressed when he glanced at Snow White.

"What's his problem?" Annie wondered aloud.

"Prince Maitland wanted to stay to court me," Snow White whispered to her, "but I'm sending him home because I overheard him talking to his friends. He cares more about my future crown than he does about me. When I marry, it will be to someone who loves me the way Liam loves you and Beldegard loves Gwendolyn."

❧

They set out soon after, with Beldegard, Gwendolyn, Liam, Annie, and Maitland riding between the knights who were escorting them. Maitland had sent his friends on ahead and he looked so dejected riding alone that after a few miles Annie took pity on him. "I'll be right back," she told Liam, and let her horse drop behind until she was riding beside the young prince.

Maitland glanced at her, then turned to look straight ahead.

"Are you upset because you're not going to be king, or because Snow White sent you away?" Annie asked him.

"Would you believe me when I say that I really liked that girl? She was sweet and innocent and didn't act like most princesses. She heard me talking to my friends about being King of Helmswood someday, but that was just talk. I didn't mean the things I said; it was just what they were expecting to hear. Beldegard is right. They aren't very good friends if I don't act like a good person because they're around. I didn't want to kill my own brother, but they had me convinced that he was never going to turn back and that the kingdom would be better off without everyone waiting for something that wasn't going to happen. I shouldn't have listened to them."

"You know, if you really like Snow White, you might still have a chance with her," said Annie. "I don't believe in love at first sight, but do you think you could love her someday? That's all she really wants."

"I really think I could!" Maitland told her, his eyes lighting up.

"She won't believe you if you just tell her that you love her, so you're going to have to prove that you do."

Maitland frowned. "And how would I do that?"

"I don't know," said Annie. "But I'm sure you can think of something." She raised her head at the sound of voices and smiled when she saw that Liam was riding back to join her.

"I need to talk to you," he told her as he reached for her reins. He held their horses in place until Maitland had ridden ahead and some of the knights had passed them.

"Is this the conversation you mentioned where you

wanted everything to be perfect?" Annie asked once their horses were moving again.

Liam nodded. "That's what I said, but I realized when you had that necklace around your neck that it would be foolish to wait. The perfect time is anytime that we're together. I realize we've know each other only a few weeks, but it seems like a lifetime to me. You're the only girl I've ever met that I want to live with for the rest of my life. I love you, Annie, and I want to marry you." The horses had slowed as Liam spoke until they were standing still.

"Hey, are you two going to dawdle back there or what?" shouted Beldegard. "There are people here who want to go home! We have things to do and lives to start living."

Annie smiled. "So do we," she said, leaning toward Liam for a kiss. "But I think our lives have already started."

Acknowledgments

I'd like to thank the authors of fairy tales long ago who inspired me with their marvelous stories, including James Orchard Halliwell-Phillips, Jacob and Wilhelm Grimm, Charles Perrault, and Robert Southey, as well as the authors whose names have been lost with the passage of time.

Snow White needs help—
so it's Princess Annie to the rescue!

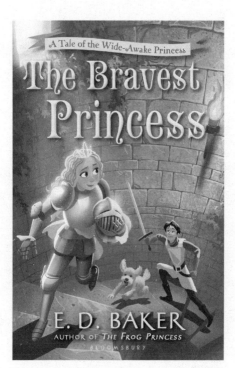

Annie still can't rest while trouble in the kingdom threatens her friend Snow White. After her evil stepmother disappears, Snow White's father wants her married off right away—but whom should she choose? How can she tell which prince is best? Read on for a selection from *The Bravest Princess*.

THEY REACHED SNOW WHITE'S CASTLE a few hours later. Annie had just crossed the drawbridge and reined her horse to a stop when a white shape shot across the courtyard, barking. "Dog!" Annie cried. She slid off her mare so she could crouch down and throw her arms around the shaggy dog's neck. A wet tongue licked the side of her face while the animal's wiggly body vibrated with joy. "How have you been? Are you happy here?" asked Annie. When the dog didn't answer, Annie pulled away and looked her in the eyes. Dog's tongue lolled out of the side of her mouth so that she almost seemed to be laughing. "Oh, right! I forgot." Annie patted the dog's head and stepped away. "You can't talk when I'm touching you."

Dog's tail wagged like a pendulum. "I'm glad you're here," the animal said in a rush. "Snow White told me you were coming. I've been waiting here for you every day." She looked past Annie to all the princes and guards. "If they came with you, they can come in. This is a very big place. It has lots of rooms. Good smells, too. I'm taking you to see Snow White. She's been waiting for you. Just you, though. The rest have to go somewhere else."

"All right," said Annie. "Lead the way." When she grabbed her mare's reins, she felt a tug on her hem and looked down.

Dog gave her a reproachful look and backed away so she could talk again. "The horse can't go with us. Snow White doesn't let horses in the castle."

"But I was just . . . ," Annie began. "Um, never mind." Handing her reins to Liam, she shrugged and said, "I'll find you later." Then she turned to follow Dog.

The last time Annie had been in the castle, Snow White's stepmother had been ruling for many years. The evil queen had neglected the castle as she'd plotted and schemed, spending little money on the buildings and letting the furnishings get rundown and dirty. Although it had been only a few weeks since Snow White had returned home and her stepmother had been locked away, repairs had already begun, and the floors and windows looked cleaner. Even now, maids scrubbed walls while seamstresses repaired tapestries.

One thing didn't seem to have changed, however. Everyone, from the lowest servant to the highest noble, had looked frightened during Annie's last visit. The unpredictable evil queen had made them wary of doing even the simplest thing that might displease her. Annie had been sure that Snow White's presence would change that and was dismayed to find that it hadn't. Footmen kept their eyes averted when Annie looked their way. A noblewoman hurried off when Annie gave her a friendly smile. When Annie glanced at a maid carrying an armload of linens, the girl ducked her head and scurried around a corner, looking so frightened that Annie almost called after her.

Confused, Annie followed Dog down the corridor and up a narrow set of stairs. She was used to people avoiding her because she might take away their magic, but this was different. Although the inhabitants of the castle seemed fearful, she didn't think it had anything to do with her.

"This is it," Dog finally said. "Snow White's room."

Dog raised her paw and tapped on the door three times. She was about to tap again when the door opened. Snow White was there, a smile lighting her face when she saw Annie.

"You came!" she cried, pulling Annie into the room. "Thank you for bringing her, Dog. Go tell the cook that I said you should have an extra-big bone!"

Dog walked off, her tail wagging again, as Snow White shut the door.

"Dog is such a dear creature, but she doesn't know how to keep secrets, and there are things I need to tell you that I don't want everyone to know," said Snow White. "Come sit over here so we can talk."

As Annie sat down on the window seat, Snow White began to fidget with a tassel on a cushion. "Cat is here as well," she finally said, glancing at Annie. "He stops by to see me every few days. I think he's just checking up on me to see if I'm all right."

"Why wouldn't you be?" asked Annie. "Snow White, what's going on?"

Snow White stood abruptly and began to pace. "I don't know what to do. You know that Father locked my stepmother, Marissa, in the dungeon when he learned that she had been putting drugs in his drink and trying to kill me. Just a few days after you and Liam left, she escaped. We still don't know how she did it, but we think she must have had help. Father is afraid that Marissa still wants to kill me. Now he's gotten the idea that if I were to marry, my prince would whisk me away to his castle and I would finally be safe from her." Snow White was wringing her hands when she turned back to Annie. "Isn't that the craziest idea you've ever heard?"

"Well...," Annie began.

"In the meantime, Father has doubled the guards. Everyone is terrified that Marissa will come back. Knowing how much she likes disguises, some think she may be here already."

"Oh my...," Annie said.

"Father sent out word to the neighboring kingdoms that I'm looking for a husband! Can you believe that? Next he'll be flying banners at the local jousting tournaments reading 'Come one, come all! Feast your eyes on the desperate princess!' I can't believe he's done this to me!"

"So," said Annie, "are you more upset because a crazy woman may be coming to kill you, or because your father was a little indiscreet about your availability?"

"Both! Although I guess the killing one is worse.... But not by much!"

"Have you heard from any princes yet?" Annie asked.

"Four. Three who I've never heard of before they arrived yesterday with their attendants, and then Maitland showed up a few hours ago. He's been sending me messages and flowers, but I couldn't bring myself to see him. Not after the last time he was here and he told his friends how much he wanted to rule my kingdom. Where is the romance in that? I want to be loved for myself, not the land my father rules or the castle we live in or the gold in our treasury. And I'm sure that after Father's announcement, that's all the other princes are going to see. Now Father is making me choose among these four princes, and he says he wants me to do it in a week's time. The thing is, I don't have any idea how to begin!"

"You actually have a few more princes to choose from. Four more came with me. There's Andreas,

Cozwald, his cousin Emilio, and Digby," Annie said, ticking them off on her fingers. "So with the four who are already here, you have eight princes."

"That just makes it worse!" wailed Snow White.

"You don't have any idea how you're going to choose?" Annie asked.

"None. I've spent all my time thinking about it, but nothing has come to me," Snow White declared. "I know some princesses send their suitors on quests, but I don't have time for that. Not if Father is giving me only a week!"

Annie thought her friend looked close to tears. "Maybe I can help. What are you looking for in a husband?"

"That's what makes it so hard," said Snow White, wringing her hands again. "They're all handsome, and they are all talented in one thing or another, and they all have excellent manners."

"And those are the most important things to you?" asked Annie.

"Well, not really," Snow White said, beginning to pace again. "He has to be honest, and brave. He also has to be compassionate. Oh, and more than anything, he has to love me for myself."

"Those are all very good traits. And how do you think you can learn if any of those things are true of these princes?"

"A contest?" asked Snow White.

"That could work," said Annie. "Do you have a quill, some ink, and a piece of parchment? I think it's time to make a list."

"I have them right here," said Snow White, gesturing toward a table in the center of the room. "You know, a contest might actually be fun."

"For us, maybe," said Annie, "but the prince who really wants to win is going to have to work hard. It may not be as much fun for him. You realize, of course, that no man is going to show you what he's really like in a contest. They'll all try to impress you with their best behavior. The princes might be very different once they relax and you really get to know them."

"I'm sure you're right," said Snow White. "I grew up in a house with seven men. None of them tried to impress me, but I do know what I don't want. I don't want a man who thinks it's funny to talk about bodily functions or who doesn't like to bathe."

"Ick!" said Annie. "How about a man who thinks mean jokes are funny? Or who loves his mother more than he loves you?"

"Or one who loves his horse more than me!" Snow White said with a laugh. "Oh, I've thought of something else I do want. I want to marry a good kisser. I've never kissed a man, except on the cheek, and I want my first real kiss to be spectacular!"

"I don't think we can make that part of the contest," said Annie.

"I know," Snow White said, though she sounded disappointed.

The princesses spent the rest of the afternoon working on the contests and lists. When they went down to supper, Annie was still thinking about the contest for honesty. They hadn't been able to come up with anything yet, but she knew how important honesty was to her, and she wanted an honest husband for Snow White.

As they entered the crowded great hall, Annie saw that King Archibald was seated at the head table. The princes had left two seats to one side of the king for Snow White and Annie. Maitland fumed as Annie introduced the four newly arrived princes to Snow White, giving Cozwald an extra-dirty look when the prince walked around the table to kiss Snow White's hand.

"Now let me introduce my other suitors to you," said Snow White as Cozwald returned to his seat. "Prince Milo is from the kingdom of Gulleer to our west."

"I understand that Gulleer's economy is based on shipping," said Liam.

"That's true," said Milo, the corners of his blue eyes crinkling when he smiled. "And we have the largest navy of any kingdom. We would like to expand our interests inland, however," he added, smiling at Snow White.

"And this is Prince Tandry," Snow White said quickly. "He comes from the mountains of Westerling."

"Isn't Westerling full of mystics?" asked Andreas.

"Yes," said Prince Tandry as he traced the grain in the tabletop with his finger. Everyone waited for him to say something else, but he didn't seem to notice.

"And this is Prince Nasheen," Snow White finally said.

"I am from the kingdom of Viramoot," said Nasheen, stroking his mustache with his index finger and thumb. He was older than the other princes, and Annie guessed that he was in his early twenties. "We're known for breeding the finest horses in all the kingdoms. Our bloodstock is second to none."

"I'm not so sure about that," said Andreas. "We breed some excellent horses in Corealis."

Annie sat back to listen while the princes got to know one another, sizing each other up as they debated who had faster horses in their stables or stronger armies in the field or fiercer dragons in their forests. Of the three princes she had never met before, Milo was sitting closest to her. She noticed that after sitting near her for a few minutes, his nose became more prominent, and his ears stuck out to the sides. When she saw that the other princes had noticed as well, she tried not to laugh at the horrified look on Prince Nasheen's face.

Tandry and Nasheen were seated so far from her that any changes in their appearances were too small to notice, but that didn't stop Nasheen from studying all the princes at her end of the table, staring longest at the ones near Annie who had changed the most. She thought that Milo might have noticed the changes in the princes near him; he seemed amused if anything. Annie didn't see any sign that Tandry had noticed, but then he seemed to be in his own world, gazing off into empty air much of the time.

Everyone turned as two serving girls carrying a huge platter between them approached the table. A roasted peacock decorated with its own feathers filled the platter, which took up the entire center of the table when the girls set it down. Everyone at the head table was served as much as they wanted before the platter was carried to the other tables.

The food kept coming after that, and Annie and Liam spent more time eating than talking. Annie had so much she wanted to tell him, but not now in front of all these people. While Snow White listened intently to the princes as they boasted, argued, and tried to impress her, Annie heard only part of the conversation as her thoughts kept wandering back to Snow White's stepmother. Marissa, the evil queen, was on the loose. Although it was possible that Marissa had fled the kingdom, she might well have stayed around, hoping to regain control of the kingdom one way or another. Annie glanced at Liam, certain that he wasn't going to like the news any more than she did.

Annie waited until supper was over and a minstrel was entertaining the diners before touching Liam's arm and whispering into his ear, "We have to talk. Let's go outside."

Pleading a need for fresh air, Annie asked the king for leave. When he granted it with a nod and a wave of his hand, she and Liam slipped from the table. They were on their way out the door when Annie saw Dog begging for scraps. Dog looked at her as if wanting an invitation to join them, but Annie shook her head and motioned for her furry friend to stay.

Once in the courtyard, they looked for a quiet place where they could talk without being overheard. They found such a place between the castle wall and the stable. When Liam pulled her into his arms to kiss her, Annie didn't protest, but after a few minutes she pulled away, saying, "I really did want to come out here to talk."

"I know," he replied with a grin. "But that doesn't mean we can't take care of more important matters first."

Annie caressed his cheek, then shook her head and stepped back a pace. "Snow White told me why she wanted me to come. Her father said that she has to get married right away because he wants her new groom to take her far away. It's for her own protection. Snow White's stepmother escaped from the dungeon, and the king is afraid she might hurt Snow White."

"When did she escape?" asked Liam.

"Only a few days after we left last time," Annie said. "They think she might have had help."

"They're right in thinking that she's dangerous, but I wonder if it's really Snow White she's after."

"Do you think Marissa might be the woman who put that green fire in my hair?" asked Annie. "It never occurred to me that it might be her. I'd thought she was still locked away. I suppose it was possible.... But why would she want to hurt me? If she wants to take over the kingdom again, wouldn't she be more likely to go after Snow White or the king?"

"Not if she wanted to get rid of you first so you couldn't come back to Helmswood to help them."

E. D. BAKER is the author of the Tales of the Frog Princess series, including *The Frog Princess*, which inspired the Disney movie *The Princess and the Frog*. Baker is also the author of the Tales of the Wide-Awake Princess series, *Fairy Wings*, *Fairy Lies*, and *A Question of Magic*. She lives with her family and many pets in Maryland.

www.talesofedbaker.com

Read all the books in the
Tales of the Frog Princess series!

Book One in the Tales of the Frog Princess

THE FROG
Princess

E.D. BAKER

Book Two in the Tales of the Frog Princess

DRAGON'S
Breath

E.D. BAKER

Book Three in this Tales of the Frog Princess

ONCE UPON
A Curse

E.D. BAKER

THE TALES OF THE FROG PRINCESS

NO PLACE
FOR
Magic

E.D. BAKER

THE TALES OF THE FROG PRINCESS

THE
SALAMANDER
Spell

E. D. BAKER

THE TALES OF THE FROG PRINCESS

THE
DRAGON
Princess

E.D. BAKER

THE TALES OF THE FROG PRINCESS

DRAGON
Kiss

E. D. BAKER

THE TALES OF THE FROG PRINCESS

A PRINCE
AMONG
Frogs

E. D. BAKER

"[A] brilliantly created world of magic and mayhem." —*VOYA*

www.talesofedbaker.com